The Anorexic Experiment

Angela Bacon Grimm

Angela Bacon Books
P.O. Box 19844
Kalamazoo, MI 49019
www.angelabaconbooks.com

ISBN-13: 978-0692873243

Cover design by Michael Grimm

Cover photo by iStock.com/badahos

Author photo by Jamie Brokus Fox

Acknowledgments

It takes a lot of people to put a book together, and I greatly appreciate all of my friends and family who have contributed to making *The Anorexic Experiment* into what it is today! Thank you to my husband Mike who was the first one to read this book, gave me editing suggestions, designed the cover, and has handled much of the "techie" side of the writing world for me for several years now. Thank you to my parents and grandparents who are always willing to read my books, provide encouragement, and help out with author events. Thank you to Stewart at the Gallagher Law Library Reference Office for your help with researching court cases and to Amy for the name "Grimm Tales." Finally, a big thank you to everyone who read *The Anorexic Experiment* in its early drafts and especially those who gave much-needed feedback (in alphabetical order)—Alyssa, Amy, Christy, Colleen, Erica, Kaitlin, and Kristin. You are all so helpful, and I am so grateful for your support!

This book is dedicated to everyone who has ever struggled with food,
whether it be restriction, binges, or otherwise.

You never realize just how many people struggle with eating disorders until you write a book about the subject. Be kind when you're talking about topics like weight and appearance with other people—you never know what kind of issues they may be dealing with. Be an encourager of good health, not of extreme dieting.

If you or someone you know is struggling with an eating disorder, please tell a parent or someone else close to you and find some advice by contacting a toll-free helpline for eating disorders:

NEDA

www.nationaleatingdisorders.org

1-800-931-2237

CHAPTER ONE

Aimee

Madelynne was missing again. Four days in a row. Aimee stared at the empty, pencil-scarred desk and chair beside her as Mrs. Schuler called out names. Even though they had sat next to each other all trimester, the only things Aimee knew about Madelynne were that she usually chewed gum, brought huge bottles of water to history class every day, and kept to herself unless talking was absolutely necessary. Madelynne needed to return soon from her illness or vacation or wherever she was because there was a partner project due in five days, and their teacher had assigned the seatmates to work together. Aimee dreaded the thought of having to do the entire thing on her own.

After class, she approached Mrs. Schuler. The plump, middle-aged woman glanced up from her planner as Aimee leaned against the desk.

"Do you know if Madelynne is sick? She's been gone all week, and we haven't been able to work on our project together."

Mrs. Schuler grimaced, her tired eyes darting away as if hiding something. "Oh, Aimee, I'm so sorry. I forgot all about this situation. I'm going to re-assign you to a different group— there will be three of you in one group. Madelynne won't be back before the project is due."

"Is she okay?" *Poor Madelynne must be seriously ill if the teachers already know she won't be back for at least a week.*

Mrs. Schuler tilted her head from side to side to indicate so-so. Her graying curls bobbed with the motion. "She will be."

"Is she sick?" Aimee knew she was probably prying too much, but she couldn't help herself.

"Aimee, I appreciate your concern, but I really can't give you any more information right now. It will be up to Madelynne to decide what to tell her classmates when she returns."

Weird. She must be either dying or pregnant, Aimee concluded as she walked to her locker.

Sara

Sara leaned against the sink as a black fog took over, narrowing her field of vision to miniscule circles directly ahead. She squeezed her eyes shut, breathed deeply, and was back to her senses after a few seconds; unfortunately, she had not been cognizant enough to release the knife in the midst of her dizzy spell. Sara winced at the sting on her thumb as blood dripped out onto the half-peeled apple she was holding. She dropped the fruit into the trash, quickly rinsed her hand and applied a bandage, and sliced a different apple onto the empty compartment of the fruit platter.

"Guys, get down here! Your breakfast is ready." Sara set a stack of buttered toast and glass pitcher of orange juice next to the fruit and slid a greasy tangle of bacon strips into the space between Aimee's plate and Cody's.

One tiny corner of bacon had flaked off onto the tablecloth, and Sara's finger covered it, the pebble of meat biting into her flesh and sticking. She drew the finger to her mouth and guiltily savored its salty taste before pouring herself a cup of coffee and easing into a cushioned seat at the table.

Her husband Dave was the first to arrive from upstairs. He bent to kiss her before taking a seat. "Morning."

She forced a smile. Apparently all was forgiven from last night. Or postponed, anyway. She was so *sick* of their recurring fights. Literally ill. She found that their heated debates (hushed so that the kids wouldn't hear) always resulted in more dizzy spells than the days Dave chose to keep silent about their problems.

"Smells good, Mom!" Cody bounded down the spiral staircase, socks surfing across hardwood as he raced to the table. He snagged half a slice of toast in one hand and a piece of bacon in the other, balancing on his left foot while pulling out his chair with the right and calling out, "Aimee, I'm gonna eat it all!" around the wad of food in his mouth.

"Cody…" Sara warned. "I'd prefer not to give you the Heimlich this morning."

"I know you're hungry, buddy, but it's your turn to pray before breakfast today, remember?" Dave had filled his own plate but had yet to take a bite.

Cody swallowed. "Sorry." He set his toast and bacon on his plate and reached for the juice. He tilted the heavy pitcher into his glass. "Gross. You got the pulpy kind again?"

Sara eyed the greasy smears that Cody's fingers left on the pitcher. "It's good for you. I'll get the other kind next time." She sipped her coffee, plastering her hands against the ceramic mug in an effort to stop their shaking. When the gesture didn't help, she finally set the mug down and clasped her hands in her lap.

Cody dug his hand into the grapes and dropped a small pile of them onto his plate. "You guys are coming to my game tonight, right?"

Sara nodded as Dave said, "Planning on it."

Aimee finally dragged herself down the stairs, wet auburn hair scattered across the back of her black suit jacket. Her clean, pale face was marred by shadows under her blue eyes and a new cluster of acne on her forehead.

"Good morning, honey." Sara smiled at her tired daughter.

"Hey." Aimee's lips barely moved. She gripped the back of a chair and slid it out, her slow movement hinting that even lifting an item weighing in at fifteen pounds was far too much manual labor for that time of day. Reaching for the juice, she splashed some into her glass and a few drops onto the pristine, spring green tablecloth.

"I'm praying!" Cody announced and completed his usual ten-second prayer of thanking God for the food.

"Why so dressed up today?" Sara asked Aimee.

Aimee dabbed half-heartedly at the juice stains. "I'm interviewing the principal." She broke off half a strip of bacon and nibbled at it.

"Wow, good for you!" Dave slathered strawberry jam onto a piece of toast. "Biggest interview yet, huh? I bet you'll be a famous journalist someday, Aimes."

Aimee shrugged and leaned one elbow on the table, eyes

drooping.

Cody belched. "Guess I have more room after all," he stated triumphantly and stuffed more toast into his mouth.

Aimee glared at him, relieving Sara of the need to say anything.

Cody, tired of apologizing for his behavior, returned the look and showed his sister the mangled mess of bread and strawberries in his mouth.

Aimee rolled her eyes, finished off her glass of orange juice, and stood, snatching a couple of grapes. "I have to go put my makeup on." She carried her dishes into the kitchen and trudged back upstairs.

Sara looked into her half-full mug and decided she didn't want any more. The acidity of the coffee was beginning to bother her stomach.

"Do you guys want anything else to eat?" She rose slowly to avoid any more potential blackouts.

Dave scraped the rest of the scrambled eggs onto his plate and shook his head.

"Nope." Cody swiped a napkin across his mouth and leaned back in his chair. "I'm full."

"Did you remember to pack your uniform in your backpack?"

"Oh, man!" Cody jumped up. "No!" He ran from the room.

Sara cleared the dishes from the table as Dave finished his meal. He finally spoke to her again as she scrubbed at Aimee's orange juice stains with dish soap and water. "What are your plans today, hon?"

"I need to set up dentist appointments for the kids. Then grocery shopping, probably." She would also spend a couple of hours working on her project, but she left that part out. Dave knew almost everything about her, but as far as she could tell, she'd been able to keep that part of her life a secret.

As she packed leftovers into the refrigerator, Sara noticed that there was one more piece of apple resting on the fruit platter. She ate it, hoping to calm her stomach by mixing the coffee with a little bit of food. By the time she had stuck the dirty dishes in the dishwasher, Aimee was downstairs again, yelling for Cody to hurry up so they wouldn't be late. Sara grabbed her purse, car keys, and a cropped denim jacket and joined her daughter in the entryway.

Aimee scrunched her hair in the mirror. "It's so frizzy today." She lifted her chin and blended a small blob of foundation she had missed at her jawline. "Do I look professional?"

"Very," Sara reassured.

Cody scrambled into their midst, pulling on Nikes and swinging his backpack over his shoulder. "I'm ready. Let's go!"

"All right. Aimee, how about if you drive today? You still need to get in twelve more hours of practice before your driving test, right?" *And I'm afraid if I drive we might get into an accident.* As long as Aimee drove on the way there, Sara would have a few more minutes to pull herself together before she needed to drive home. She handed her daughter the keys.

Aimee

Aimee crossed her legs and slumped in an ugly orange chair, looking over the page of interview questions and tapping the end of her pen against her cheek as she waited for the school secretary to send her back to Principal Owens' office. It was an honor to interview the principal, but *ughhh*. This article was going to be so boring to write.

Creeping a hand up to the collar of her blazer, Aimee made sure nothing was sticking up that was not supposed to be and ended up playing with her diamond necklace, a gift from Mom and Dad for her fifteenth birthday. She twisted the pendant back and forth between pointer finger and thumb, biting her lip and wondering whether she should reword her first question.

"Aimee?" The elderly secretary, Mrs. Collins, pushed a stack of papers out of the way and leaned across her desk. The movement slipped one of the top buttons out of its hole on her ill-fitted white blouse, and Aimee barely caught herself from making a face at the wrinkled skin and cleavage that suddenly appeared. "That was Mr. Owens I was just talking to on the phone. It's going to be a few more minutes, and then you can go back there to talk with him."

"While I wait, could I get a comment from you about the principal?"

Mrs. Collins cringed and then sighed. She ran a hand down the back of her short hair and cleared her throat.

What on earth was that about?

"Sure, I guess that would be all right." She looked as though Aimee had just asked her to eat a rotten egg.

Maybe Mrs. Collins and Mr. Owens aren't getting along well? "Okay, what is your opinion about what Mr. Owens is doing for this school? Do you think he's improved it in the year and a half he's worked here?"

Mrs. Collins looked up to the ceiling and pondered her answer so long that Aimee thought the woman might be about to renege on her agreement to provide a statement.

"I think…I think he really cares about the kids and wants to do what's best for the school," she replied vaguely.

"Any specific examples of great things he's done for the school?"

The phone rang at that moment, and Mrs. Collins looked thrilled to answer it. She held up a finger. "Just a moment, dear."

Mr. Owens walked into the office while his secretary was still on the phone. He held out his hand to Aimee, and Aimee made sure to use her firmest handshake.

"You must be Aimee Jones."

She nodded. "I am. Thank you for agreeing to meet with me today."

He smiled. "Of course. Sorry about your wait."

Once inside his office, Aimee took a seat in a chair that was the identical twin of the orange one she had just vacated. Mr. Owens' chair, on the other hand, looked to be brand new. Aimee could smell the leather.

He sat down behind his desk and leaned back, drumming his fingers on the tabletop. "So what's your first question?"

It was clear over the course of the interview that the principal was distracted. Aimee couldn't quite figure out what was going on; she knew that he constantly had a lot of work to do to keep the school running, but the phone wasn't ringing or anything. If he would have focused, they would have been finished in fifteen or twenty minutes. Instead, he rambled on with stories about topics unrelated to her questions, and she was stuck in his office for nearly forty-five minutes. Aimee felt discouraged at the prospect of digging out a few good quotes from this mess of an interview. She hoped Mrs. Collins would have a good statement for her now that she'd had almost an hour to think about her answer to Aimee's question. *I can't believe I spent so much time deciding what to wear so I'd look professional today. Mr. Owens isn't acting professional at all.*

Unfortunately, when Aimee exited Mr. Owens' office, Mrs. Collins refused to look up and quickly began to dial a phone number. *Forget that quote. Whatever.*

She headed to journalism. Mrs. Bennett always gave them some time in class on Tuesdays to work on their current assignment, so Aimee would have some time to organize the information Mr. Owens had given her. Before allowing the students free reign of the computers, though, Mrs. Bennett had an announcement.

"We have one more normal paper to put together after this one, and then the paper at the beginning of April is going to be a special issue. I am not going to assign topics. I want you to pick a topic on your own—an appropriate topic, please—and write an article about it. If it's not appropriate, it won't make it into the newspaper, and it won't count as one of your four required articles for the trimester. Since you have about a month from now to finish it, I'm going to give you two weeks to figure out your topic and start writing an outline for your article. You'll need to bring your outline to class on March 8th."

Oooohhhh, this sounds fun. So many of Mrs. Bennett's topics were less than interesting. Aimee looked forward to the creativity allowed in this assignment.

"Before we focus on that, though, we need to decide on assignments for the next paper. I'm going to pass out the list of topics, and let's make some decisions quickly so that you'll have time left to work on your current articles."

Aimee scanned the list and circled the ones that interested her. The most fascinating idea on the sheet was labeled "Josh Trudeau—seventeen-year-old millionaire." His name sounded slightly familiar. She raised her hand when Mrs. Bennett asked if anyone had any questions. "Who is Josh Trudeau? Does he

9

live around here?"

"Josh Trudeau was born in our city but moved to New York a couple of years ago. He invented something last year that's become a big hit and is now making a ton of money off of it. It would have to be a phone interview instead of in-person."

That's why he sounds familiar. Aimee vaguely remembered someone named Josh Trudeau who had been a couple grades ahead of her in elementary school. She didn't recall seeing him for the past several years, though, so he must have transferred schools even before moving to New York.

"Is he cute?" One of Aimee's classmates, Kirsten, smiled mischievously as she asked the question. A couple of other girls in the class giggled.

Aimee rolled her eyes. Kirsten never took their assignments seriously.

Mrs. Bennett sighed. "I don't know, Kirsten. Do you want this topic?"

"Yeah, I'll take it."

Disappointed that her first choice was now eliminated, Aimee searched through the list again. She didn't see anything else that looked out of the ordinary from what she typically wrote for the paper, so maybe she would sit this one out. They only had to write four articles per trimester, and she'd already completed three.

After journalism and geometry, Aimee joined her best friends in line for pizza in the cafeteria. As they waited, she complained about her history class from the previous afternoon and the mystery of her missing partner. "I know Mrs. Schuler didn't forget to tell me on purpose, but I feel like she should give me an extension now."

Meghan looked at her with wide eyes and appeared to be

fighting to keep her mouth shut the longer Aimee talked. "I know what happened to Madelynne!"

"Of course you do." Coralee grabbed a tray and raised her eyebrows at their friend. Meghan spent much more of her time socializing than she did working on assignments or paying attention in class.

Meghan stuck out her tongue at Coralee. "She's staying at a clinic for eating disorders."

"How did you hear that?" Aimee selected two slices of pizza and a little container of carrots and dip, following Coralee. She ate a quick bite of pizza, unable to wait any longer to satisfy her hunger pangs.

"Her brother and my brother are on the basketball team together. Scott was mad because her brother missed their last game so the whole family could drive down to a clinic in Arizona to drop Madelynne off."

Sounds legit. Meghan's information was correct eighty percent of the time. "How long does someone go to a clinic like that for?"

Meghan shrugged and brushed some crumbs off of the countertop in front of her. "No idea. My guess is that it's more than just a week or two, though, since the whole family took her together instead of just her mom or dad dropping her off alone. She was in the hospital for a weekend last month, I heard. She was having heart problems from not eating enough."

"Wow." Aimee felt sorry she had been angry with Madelynne for not participating in their partner project. Obviously the girl had other issues that took precedence.

As they found an empty table and moved on to other topics, Aimee scarfed through the rest of her pizza, the vegetables, a thick piece of chocolate cake, and a can of pop.

She had a few minutes left before class to study for a biology test, so she dismissed herself from the table during a lull in her friends' conversation and walked out to her locker. She enjoyed the authoritative click of her high heels against the cold linoleum; uncomfortable as they were, the shiny black shoes looked great with her blazer and were worth the blisters Aimee knew she would develop by the time school let out for the day.

Even though many of the students were still at lunch, a few gathered supplies from their lockers. One girl, pale and scrawny, stepped out of the women's restroom a few feet in front of Aimee and mumbled an apology for nearly running into her. Aimee watched the girl skitter toward a locker, head down. She appeared to be as skinny as Madelynne had been looking the past few weeks. Aimee instantly had an idea for her next article, one that should catch the attention of many students. She smiled.

Bingo.

CHAPTER TWO

Aimee

Aimee could hardly wait to get home from school to start researching. She wanted to write something on anorexia—something that was not just the typical stats and please-seek-help-if-you-fit-these-five-symptoms informative articles that appeared periodically in teen magazines. Over the course of the afternoon, she had quietly made plans while pretending to listen to her geography teacher drone on about the weather in South America and while waiting for the rest of her class to finish their biology test. She was going to do a three-day experiment and live as if she were an anorexic, consequently experiencing on a small scale what anorexics had to do in order to keep their eating habits a secret and discovering whether other people noticed her diet change or not. Her hope was that the article would give the students more compassion for those who had eating disorders and would help them to recognize any problematic behaviors that their friends might exhibit.

Her excitement about this experiment and article was

slightly dampened by the fact that deep down, she knew Mrs. Bennett would think the temporary extreme dieting was too dangerous for Aimee's health.

But it was just three days. And she didn't even have to tell Mrs. Bennett the topic of her article for another fourteen days.

So, basically, Aimee could do the experiment now, without telling anyone (it would make it more authentic, anyway—see if people noticed), and then deal with the consequences later if Mrs. Bennett was angry. At that point she would be finished with the experiment and could write a unique article, and hopefully her teacher would see that the article should be published in the school paper.

Aimee's mom was waiting for her in the car, reading *Woman's World* to pass the time. The scent of Sara's favorite air freshener, pine, wafted out as Aimee swung open the passenger's side door and dumped her heavy bookbag on the floor before sitting. "Hey, Mom. Are we going to Cody's game now?"

Sara tossed the magazine into the backseat and started the car. "It's up to you. I told him I would come, but I can drop you off at home first if you aren't interested."

Aimee hadn't exactly been planning to start her experiment already, but this did give her the perfect opportunity. Instead of waiting for a new day to start, she could run the experiment for 72 hours—start now and finish on Friday. *If I don't go to the game, I can tell Mom that I ate something while they were gone when she tries to get me to eat supper later.* "Home, please."

A few minutes later, Aimee unlocked their front door and waved to her mom as she backed out of the driveway to head for the soccer arena. She suddenly thought of the snacks she would miss by not going to the game; even though she didn't care much for soccer, the junk food served at the concession stand was enjoyable every once in a while—especially when it had been over three hours since lunch, and she knew she was not going to be able to eat much the next few days. Her mouth instantly salivated, and her heart rate sped up a little at the thought of the salty taste of nachos and cheese. *My word, Aimee, calm down! You can eat nachos next week.*

She slammed her hand down on the spotless kitchen island, willing herself to be calm and level-headed. In order to stick to this diet, she needed to approach her experiment from a logical standpoint, rather than from an emotional, starving sort of mentality. *What can I eat that would be low-calorie?* Aimee peered into the refrigerator, eyeing the leftover fruit from that morning. Fruit didn't have that many calories. She wasn't sure how many each type of fruit had; she just knew fruit didn't have many calories in general. Pulling out the Tupperware container, Aimee decided she would begin her article research by looking up the number of calories in grapes and strawberries.

She tucked the plastic dish under her arm and toted her backpack upstairs to her bedroom. Gently kicking open the door, she was greeted by the sight of her green comforter falling off her unmade bed; a small, squishy pile containing last night's pajamas and yesterday's school clothes; and the sound of her tower fan calmly whooshing air into the room. She couldn't stand sleeping without the fan on but almost always forgot to turn it off before leaving each day.

Aimee slumped into her swivel chair, threw an empty plastic water bottle and a folder onto the bed behind her to make some space on the desk, and popped open the plastic lid on her snack. Their dog, Treasure, poked his head into her room and walked over for a head rub. She stroked his long fur with one hand and waited impatiently while her computer warmed up, sticking a slick grape in her mouth every ten seconds or so with the other hand. Before she knew it, the grapes were gone. Just a couple of small strawberries lingered in the transparent bottom of the dish, and she hadn't even typed her search into Google yet.

Man, I'm bad at this diet thing, she thought guiltily, wiping her damp hand on her pants before resting her fingers on the keyboard.

Scrolling through the first page of results, Aimee's eyes landed on a blog that contained the words *grapes*, *strawberries*, and *calories*, making it fit her search terms. The name of the website was pro_ana525.com. *Ana? Ana must be the blogger's name?* She didn't know but figured if the website contained calorie information, she was all about it.

Aimee was astonished to find the entire blog was devoted to service as a food journal of sorts. She quickly figured out that "ana" stood for "anorexic," as each of the five entries shown on the main page of the site listed small amounts of food, paragraphs above and below the lists detailing the girl's weight fluctuations and exclamations of guilt over the foods she had indulged in. Despite the girl's apparent shame from allowing herself to eat more than she had originally planned at the beginning of each of the days, she had not eaten more than 800 calories in any single entry. Three days ago she'd only eaten 75 calories over the course of twenty-four hours. That particular entry was full of rejoicing and encouragement for other anorexic girls who might be reading her blog. "Keep at it, girls! I know you can do it!"

Aimee remembered reading something in the past about minimum daily caloric intake. She didn't remember the exact count but thought it was 1500 or 2000 calories and wrote a note to look up that information later to include in her article. She clicked on the link for the 12 comments left on yesterday's entry. Girls with names like soon_to_be_Barbie and toomuchfat419 had left brief notes, such as "I wish I could be as disciplined as you! Ana love!" with accompanying profile pictures of super-thin celebrities.

She spent the next hour paging through different girls' websites, all with either bulimia or anorexia or a little of both. The ones Aimee spent the most time reading were blogs which provided tips on how to resist food and which foods contained the fewest calories but still tasted okay. She learned about all sorts of diets and "thinspo"—inspirational pictures of ultra-thin women, mainly celebrities, to help those with eating disorders not to give up on their diets. She wrote down various ideas to help her in her experiment, so engrossed in her research that she forgot about the two strawberries left in the bowl. When it came time to start her history homework, Aimee had a little more willpower and knowledge to help her, and she felt good about herself for dumping the two tiny, red enemies into the kitchen trash. Small victories counted. *It's all about the experiment.*

Sara

Sara huddled on the wooden bleachers wrapped in her husband's large jacket, nursing a bottled water. Despite the fact that it was indoor soccer, she was still freezing. Sara looked over at the scoreboard every five minutes or so, keeping track of how much longer she had to sit through this game.

"Honey, you want anything to eat?" Dave crumpled the trash left over from his hot dog. "I'm going to go get some popcorn."

"No, I'm fine. Thanks." Sara smiled at him briefly, pulling the jacket tighter and holding her water up to show it wasn't gone yet.

"You sure?" Dave glanced from the bottle to his wife, staring at her extra long. "Did you have a big lu—"

"Yeah," Sara interrupted. *Let's not get into an argument in front of all these people.*

"Okay." Dave shrugged, feet thudding against the bleachers as he made his way down to the floor.

Setting the bottle of water beside her feet, Sara focused on the next steps she needed to complete for her project in an effort to drown out thoughts of how much it bothered her that Dave was worried about her habits. When Dave didn't talk about her health, she was able to pretend she was a normal person—a normal wife and mother. But when he brought the topic up (seemingly every day now), she was forced to face the fact that it wasn't normal to feel like she was going to pass out several times a day. Then, when she would delve deeper into that thought process, she would begin to worry about their marriage and whether Dave might be thinking of divorcing her. As often as she argued with him, she really did want to preserve their marriage—not just for the kids' sake, but also because she loved Dave. She had loved him for twenty years and couldn't imagine what life would be like without him.

Tears welled up in her blue eyes, and she reached for her purse to give herself an excuse to turn away from the crowd so no one would notice. She dug out her cell phone as one tear managed to slide out and down her cheek. Horrified, Sara tilted her head forward so her hair could hide her face and scrolled through her email. She spent the rest of the game deleting old messages from her inbox and occasionally glanced up to check on the status of Cody's game.

CHAPTER THREE

Aimee

Aimee combed through her wet hair in front of a foggy mirror, stomach empty and begging her to listen to her mother's call to come to breakfast. She had nearly given in to eating several times last night, but after walking to the well-stocked kitchen and staring into cupboards, she eventually just sucked on a peppermint and spent some time on her article about Mr. Owens. Today she was determined to count her calories, the way somebody who actually had an eating disorder would do. She was even thinking about starting her own food blog to keep track of calories—perhaps that would let her into the "in" crowd and allow her to have some conversations with those in the anorexic culture.

Since she didn't need to save time for breakfast, Aimee finished getting ready for school and then lay down on the carpet for some sit-ups. Someone knocked briefly, and Cody burst into the room as she sat up for the sixteenth time.

"Aimee! Mom wants to know if you want any French

toast. It has whipped cream!" He reached around behind her as she sat up again and rubbed her hair quickly several times, causing much of the top layer to stick straight out, full of static. He left his hand near her head for a few seconds, and she knew he was making the strands suspended in mid-air dance up and down.

Aimee glared at him. "Thanks a lot, Cody. No, I don't want any French toast."

She found it difficult to concentrate in first period. Her stomach growled loudly, and Aimee thought she could almost taste the high-calorie, sugar-filled breakfast she had smelled at her house that morning. *It hasn't even been a whole day yet, and already I'm struggling with not eating. How do anorexic girls do this all the time? I hope it gets easier.*

After taking a pop quiz, the rest of the class period was spent discussing proper grammar (and the lack of it in the papers they'd turned in last week). Aimee, who felt fairly comfortable in the realm of commas and semicolons, tuned out and drew pictures of pizza and ice cream cones in the margins of her notebook. Even though she knew she couldn't eat much at lunch, she was eagerly awaiting the chance to put *something* in her stomach in a little over an hour. The school cafeteria provided a salad bar, so she figured that would be the best route for her today. Aimee wasn't the biggest fan of vegetables, but they were definitely low-calorie. She'd steer clear of the shredded cheese for sure and try to stay away from the dressing. Sounded boring but at least it would make her stomach stop grumbling for a bit.

Third period absolutely *dragged*. Her stomach growled again, even louder this time, and the guy sitting next to her laughed when it did. She blushed and focused on her worksheet.

Finally, lunch arrived. Aimee reluctantly bypassed the pizza and chicken nuggets with their tantalizing smells and walked up to the salad bar. Most of the lettuce was wilted and turning brown, and the rest of the other raw vegetables didn't look so hot, either. She sorted through the lettuce with the plastic tongs, pushing aside the pieces that looked as though they'd been sitting out in the open air all week and picked out a few leaves that didn't look quite as bad as the rest. Initially, no one else had been in line for the salad bar, but now a few stragglers were beginning to step up. The girl directly behind her cleared her throat when Aimee failed to move down to the cucumbers and carrots after an acceptable amount of time.

Aimee knew she was taking a long time, but seriously, couldn't this girl see how awful the lettuce looked? She plopped the tongs down into the lettuce and glanced up at the girl, digging for something to say that wouldn't be completely rude but would make a point at the same time. To her pleasant surprise, the throat-clearer was the too-skinny girl Aimee had seen in the hall the previous day. Her anger dissolving, Aimee realized she could probably learn a lot from this girl that she might be able to use for her experiment, and she smiled. "Hey! Sorry it's taking me so long. The lettuce just looks so bad today."

"It takes away some of your hunger, doesn't it?" The girl gave a bit of a smile. "The lettuce rarely looks good. The salad bar is totally a safe zone for people who are trying to count calories. If you tell yourself you can only have the salad bar, and then even the salad doesn't look good, it's easier to talk yourself out of pigging out." She placed a few pieces of lettuce on her plate and then loaded on sliced cucumbers.

"Wow, you must really like cucumbers," Aimee said, hoping to keep the conversation going.

"They're all right. There's less than 50 calories in an entire cucumber; isn't that amazing?"

"Really." Aimee tucked that piece of information into her memory. She had only selected two slices of cucumber for her own plate. It would have looked a little weird for her to backtrack to the cucumbers now, directly after the girl had told her that, but she would remember that fact for tomorrow's lunch.

"Jenna, hi!" A red-headed sophomore from Aimee's history class slid into line and started talking to the calorie-counting girl.

By the time she reached the end of the salad bar, Aimee was shocked to see that Jenna's plate was much fuller than her own. Sure, nearly half the plate was cucumbers, but much of the rest of it was bits and pieces of other items that Aimee had avoided, thinking they were too high-calorie for someone pretending to be "anorexic" to eat. *I'm getting salad dressing, then,* she consoled her empty stomach. It would be her reward for cutting back so much on her food. Maybe she had been wrong about Jenna—maybe the girl didn't have an eating disorder after all.

She realized as she dripped the dressing onto her food just how small of a portion the salad took up. It barely filled a third of the plate. *This is going to look really weird to my friends.* Normally her plate was nearly overflowing.

Well, if anyone asked, she'd just say she wasn't feeling well. Or something along those lines. Aimee hated lying, but this experiment was only for three days. When her article came out everybody would know what she'd been up to, anyway.

The table where Aimee and her friends normally sat was conveniently close to where Jenna was sitting. *Maybe I can pick up some tips by observation.* For now, she would just try to eat slowly and savor every wilted bite.

Meghan and Coralee were deeply involved in conversation when Aimee took a seat by them. She breathed in an excited sigh of relief at the thought of getting to put some food in her stomach and tuned them out as she focused in on her salad. She attempted to take small bites to make the meal last longer, but everything was gone within three minutes. Aimee twisted the tines of her fork around in some dressing left on her plate, debating whether it would look weird to take a bite entirely made up of dressing. She glanced at the next table over. Jenna still had a fairly full plate of food and was laughing and talking with her own friends.

"Aimee? Aimee!"

She looked over at Meghan, whose eyebrows were furrowed.

"Are you okay? You're so quiet today." The girl's long, dark hair hung in curls about her shoulders, and the bright colors of her dangly beaded earrings stood out in stark contrast to the thick hair. The earrings tangled into curls as she tilted her head in curiosity at Aimee. "Are you watching a guy?"

Aimee's cheeks reddened at having been caught ignoring her friends, and she struggled for a response. "No, just...I...I don't feel well today." Guilt pricked at her conscience. She had ended up using her lie, and she hadn't even been asked about the lack of food on her plate.

"Oh." Meghan paused to dunk a chicken nugget in some ranch. "Are you staying this afternoon, or are you going to call your mom to come pick you up?" She took a bite.

Aimee eyed the other half of the chicken nugget on her friend's fork with longing. "Planning to stay." That statement was truthful, at least.

"Okay, Aimee, I need your opinion." Coralee's green eyes

sparkled with excitement. "This morning, in first hour, Adam Warsaw asked me to next month's dance, and I told him I would let him know tomorrow. *Then*, in second period, Logan Schmitt asked me to the dance. I told him I would let him know tomorrow, too. Who should I pick?"

"Well, who do you like more?" Aimee wiped her mouth with her napkin, choosing to focus in on her friend instead of the fact that her stomach screamed to be filled.

"That's the thing. I'm still hoping Rob will ask me, but it's not looking good. So, when it comes to Adam and Logan, I'm really sort of neutral toward both. They're nice and are okay-looking, but I wasn't expecting either of them to ask me to the dance."

"So...Rob would have to ask you today, otherwise you'll need to pick either Adam or Logan because you said you'd let them know tomorrow." Aimee's gaze momentarily pulled away from her friend when someone walked by with a large, cheese-oozing slice of pizza. The smell of dough and greasy pepperoni made her mouth salivate. *Oooooh, I want that so much!*

"Well, yeah." Coralee put her hands on her head. "Oh my gosh, you guys, this is a lot of pressure! What should I do?"

Meghan rolled her eyes. "Just be glad two people asked you already and pick one of them. Don't wait around for Rob. He's a jerk."

Aimee silently agreed with Meghan but tried to soften her approach. "Coralee, you never know, there's always the chance that Rob could still ask you out, but there are also other dances he could ask you to. So I think you should probably pick Adam or Logan and stop worrying about it. Just because you pick one of them for this dance doesn't mean you're giving up on dating Rob for all of time."

Coralee nodded. "Okay, you guys. You're right."

Lunch ended five minutes later, and the three parted ways to head off to class. It wasn't until halfway through geometry that Aimee realized her friends never even seemed to notice that she was barely eating. Maybe being anorexic was going to be easier than she'd expected.

After school, Aimee swung by the principal's office to clarify some of the stats he'd given her in their interview so she could finish her article on him that evening. Mrs. Collins sighed when she looked up to see Aimee haunting the office again. "What can I do for you?"

Aimee gave the woman a tight smile, annoyed that the secretary seemed unable to be kind despite the fact that Aimee had been nothing but polite to her through this whole process. "I just need to double-check a few things Mr. Owens told me yesterday. It'll take two minutes. May I speak with him?"

"He's already left for the day." Mrs. Collins pursed her lips and stared at Aimee, obviously hoping Aimee would take the hint and leave.

Aimee was not about to include information in her article that she was not certain was absolutely correct. "Do you think I could email him my questions?"

The secretary considered this idea, and Aimee could almost hear her thinking, *That seems easier than taking a message and having to tell him tomorrow.*

"Sure." Mrs. Collins ripped a Post-it off her desk and wrote down Mr. Owens' email address. "I'm not sure if he'll have time to get back to you right away."

"Okay. Thank you." Aimee accepted the yellow paper and backed out of the office as quickly as she could.

CHAPTER FOUR

Aimee

Aimee had hoped to eat some vegetables at dinner, but her mom, citing a headache, retreated to bed as soon as she had picked them up from school. So Dad was in charge of supper, which meant pizza. When he arrived at the house with an extra-large supreme pizza that smelled amazing and further reminded Aimee of the pizza she'd longed for at lunch, she plopped a slice onto a paper plate and disappeared into her room while her dad and Cody settled into the living room with their dinner to watch a baseball game.

"Homework, kiddo?" her dad asked when she started up the stairs.

"Uh…yeah." She genuinely did have some homework, but it technically wasn't enough to warrant skipping out on eating with the family.

Aimee sat at her computer, eyeing the pizza. She had opened up a website that listed calorie counts, and so before she took a bite, she figured she should probably total up her calories for the day. From what she could figure, she'd only consumed 250 calories all day, but was that good enough compared to what a real anorexic would eat? She looked up five different blogs to see other girls' calorie counts from the previous day. Everyone seemed to have eaten more than 250 calories per day in their recent posts, except for one girl who had consumed nothing except Diet Coke and water two days in a row.

Aimee looked closer at the blog of someone who had recently eaten just over 300 calories in one day to see whether she typically ate that little or if yesterday had been a particularly low count for her. The blogger was clearly devoted to her site, *Shh—I Don't Eat*, as she typically posted two to three times each week and had been for many months. Aimee skimmed a handful of posts and realized this blogger was most likely an adult, not a teenager. The tone seemed more mature, and the posts contained fewer grammatical errors than many of the other sites. She wrote down the name of the blog to check on again later.

*What to do, what to do…*She was concerned that if she gave in and ate one bite that she would then proceed to eat the entire slice. From what she could gather online, the whole slice would be worth at least 250 calories, doubling that day's intake in just a few moments of guilty pleasure. She had done so well all day. Aimee picked off a chunk of green pepper covered in pepperoni grease and popped it in her mouth. She nearly moaned in delight but then scolded herself, *This is only temporary. In just a couple more days you can eat whatever and whenever you want. Control yourself!*

She set the plate of pizza across the room, on top of her neatly-made bed (avoiding breakfast meant she had actually had time to clean up a little in her room that morning), and draped the temptation with a napkin to disguise the smell. Aimee then turned her back on the pizza and sat down at her desk to find something to watch on Netflix. Tomorrow she would try consuming only Diet Coke and water, like the girl in one of the blogs she was following. It was her last full day of this anorexic experiment—a single day of just liquids shouldn't hurt her. Plus, it would give her the "true experience" of a real anorexic and should definitely add some dimension to her article.

At the end of her show, Aimee logged onto Twitter and noticed she had a new direct message from Kirsten.

Aimee, I have a favor to ask. I can't meet with Josh Trudeau on Friday because Trey Nichols asked me out on a date for Friday! Mrs. Bennett is going to kill me if I flake out on another article. But as long as I get someone else to cover it, she can't possibly be *that* mad, because last time the main thing that bothered her was that she didn't have enough articles to fill the paper. Anyway, would you be willing to meet with him Friday and write the article for me? I'd owe you big time. Let me know as soon as possible, k? Thanks!

Aimee sighed and rolled her eyes. Kirsten was notorious for trying to get people to cover her newspaper assignments. She had never asked Aimee before, but Aimee had overheard plenty of their other classmates complaining about it. She started to type back "No" but thought about it some more and decided that maybe this was a great opportunity. She had wanted this assignment and had been disappointed when

31

Kirsten grabbed it first.

Okay, Kirsten, I'll do it. Where are you supposed to meet Josh and what time?

Kirsten responded immediately with a bazillion smiley faces. Aimee almost reconsidered her offer at the sight of all those annoying emojis cluttering up her screen.

Thanks, Aimee, you're the best! I'm supposed to meet him at the coffee shop on James Street at 4:30 Friday afternoon. Here's his phone number: 321-8467. THANK YOU! I couldn't believe it when Trey asked me out, he's so hot! I was scared that if I turned him down, he wouldn't give me a second chance, you know?

Aimee *didn't* know. She was rarely asked out by any guys, and the only time she had had a date to anything was to a middle school dance. Her dad had nearly killed that thirteen-year-old boy when Aimee announced she had a date.

Right. Okay, will you call Josh tomorrow and let him know about the change in plans?

Aimee typed "Josh Trudeau" into the search section on Twitter while waiting for Kirsten's response. It would help if she knew what the guy looked like so she didn't approach the wrong stranger in the coffee shop on Friday.

Sure, I'll take care of it. Thanks again, Aimee!

There was a ridiculous number of Josh Trudeaus, so Aimee turned to Google instead and typed in a few more search terms to narrow things down. Several images of him popped up, and she smiled. Kirsten, who had been so concerned in class about whether Josh Trudeau was hot or not, must not have researched him since receiving her assignment. If she had, she definitely would have picked to meet with this millionaire for coffee rather than hang out with Trey Nichols, whose good looks quite honestly didn't hold a candle to this guy. Aimee suddenly found herself growing nervous about the interview and pondering what she would wear. She didn't care much for the guys in her high school, but this guy, even though a teenager, was mature for his age and *ran a business!* She needed to plan out her interview questions carefully so as to sound equally professional and mature. Anorexic blogs forgotten, Aimee turned instead to researching Josh's life and carefully crafted several questions to ask him over coffee on Friday.

The slice of pizza cooled off quickly, the cheese growing rubbery and the splash of sauce on the plate turning into a fine red crust. It was completely unappetizing by the time Aimee returned to it, and she had no qualms about wrapping it in napkins and tissues and dumping it in the bathroom trash.

She had emailed Mr. Owens from her phone on the way home from school, so she checked to see if he'd responded yet and was initially delighted to find an email from him. Her excitement turned to confusion as she read the message, though.

Amie,
Yess, those numbrs are Okay. ☺ ;)
Greg Onews

Aimee re-read the email five times, trying to figure out what had happened. Besides the other errors in the email, her principal had even misspelled his own name? Could it be some kind of massive auto-correct mistake? Had she sent her message to the wrong email address? She double-checked the paper Mrs. Collins had given her.

Nope, she'd sent it to the right place. Her principal was definitely the one responding to her. *A winky face? Really?* Was he ill or something? Well, at least she could finish her article now. She'd worry later about what had been going through Mr. Owens' head when he'd typed out that email.

*****

On Thursday, Aimee felt a little woozy when she first sat up to get out of bed. A bad start to her water-and-Diet-Coke-only day. She contemplated changing her plans to include a bit of fruit or something solid but then decided to stick with her original goal. Other girls did this *all the time*. She only had to do it for one day. Tomorrow she'd eat a small amount of food during the day and then could eat a normal-sized meal at dinnertime. Her "torture" was almost over.

Her jeans felt a bit looser than normal when she stopped feeling dizzy and stood up to put them on. *Wow, that happened fast.* She hadn't expected to see results from her diet already. *This must be why girls get pulled in to eating disorders so easily.* She lifted her shirt up to the band of her bra and stood sideways in front of the full-length mirror on the back of her bedroom door.

Sure enough, her stomach, although it had been fairly flat before this experiment, looked flatter than normal. Her shirt hung much more smoothly on her body as well. Aimee could see how other girls might be tempted to continue with something like this, but she enjoyed food too much. She couldn't wait to eat a regular meal tomorrow. Besides, she was fairly thin to begin with—thinner than probably at least 50% of the other high school girls, so she didn't have anything to worry about. But still…she lifted up her shirt and admired her flat stomach again. Well, maybe after she returned to eating normally, she would devote more time to ab exercises and could achieve this look without starving herself.

Mom called her to breakfast as she ran a brush through her hair. *Water and Diet Coke day. Water and Diet Coke day.* Mom would never approve of just pop for breakfast. Heck, she wouldn't approve of pop with breakfast at all. *Well*…Aimee pulled her hair tie out and plugged in her curling iron. She wouldn't make time for breakfast, then. She would let her mother and Cody keep calling her downstairs and keep telling them she was almost ready. At the last minute, when it was time to leave for school, she would slip downstairs and make excuses about how she didn't have time to eat because she would be late for school.

Sure enough, over the next thirty minutes, Mom called her two more times, Cody another time, and then Cody came to bang on her door like he always did when she was taking too long. She opened her door and showed Cody that she was only halfway through curling her thick hair. "I have to finish this first, Codes."

He snickered and made a horrible face. "You look like a monster!"

Aimee slammed her bedroom door and returned to the mirror. Her curls poofed out from one side of her head, and the other half was flat and fuzzy around her face. At this rate, she didn't know if she legitimately would be ready on time for school. At least her breakfast excuse would be truthful.

"Time to go!" Mom called out ten minutes later. Aimee hurriedly curled a few more stray hairs, bobby-pinned the top section back, and grabbed her bookbag. When she walked downstairs, Mom had already put most of the breakfast stuff away but turned to her. "Aimee, do you want to take something to eat in the car?"

"No, we don't have time, but thanks!" She hurried to the garage before her mother could ask any more questions or try to persuade her to eat.

Sara followed Cody out the door a moment later and jangled the keys. "Aimee, do you want to drive?"

Aimee had already settled into the front passenger seat. "Ummmm, sure." She wanted to be able to take her driving test soon, and the only way that would happen was if she completed her practice hours. She bounced out of her seat, grasped the door a moment when she felt slightly dizzy again, shook the feeling off, and slid into the driver's side. Her mom took the passenger seat. Cody chattered away in the back, going on and on about his spelling test and some new video game coming out that he wanted their parents to buy him for his birthday. He tried to bribe their mother into buying it for him sooner if he earned 100% on his spelling test that week.

Aimee worked hard at concentrating on the road in front of her. Normally she liked to drive, but this morning, with no food in her stomach and dizziness coming and going, she wished she'd told her mom she didn't want to drive today. Thankfully, it was less than a ten-minute drive to school. She managed to block out Cody's incessant talking after a couple of minutes and didn't even realize when her mom asked her a question.

"Aimee." Mom's tone implied she had already said something to Aimee, and Aimee hadn't responded.

"Sorry, Mom. What?"

"I said you look nice. Do you have something extra important at school today?"

"Uhhhh, no. Just felt like curling my hair today for something different." She chose a parking spot near the front door of Cody's junior high. Cody said bye, jumped out, and Aimee continued on to her high school. When she stopped at a red light, she glanced over at her mom to say something and paused.

Her mom was leaning her head against the back of the seat, eyes closed.

"Mom? Do you feel okay today?"

"Yeah, I just didn't sleep well last night because of my migraine. The migraine's mostly gone now, though, so that's good." She smiled but didn't open her eyes.

"Good." Aimee's stomach growled. She sucked it in, trying to quiet it down.

"You should've eaten breakfast."

"Yeah." Aimee didn't say anything else the rest of the way to school. She didn't want to talk about food.

As soon as Aimee walked in the doors, she sought out a vending machine. She had five minutes before class started to get a Diet Coke to help fill her stomach. There were only two people ahead of her. She pushed her quarters into the slot as quickly as she could and felt hopeful at the sound of the can rolling down to the depository at the bottom of the machine. She fished it out, relishing the feel of the cold, round can in her hand.

Mrs. Bennett was walking by when Aimee turned around. "Oh, I wanted to let you know that Kirsten gave me her assignment on Josh Trudeau. He's going to be in town tomorrow, so it won't have to be a phone interview after all."

"Next time ask me before you take one of Kirsten's assignments. She needs to write more articles to fill her quota for this trimester, otherwise she's not going to pass my class."

"Okay. I'll see you later, Mrs. Bennett."

"Bye, Aimee."

The Diet Coke was three-fourths of the way gone by the time Aimee was ten minutes into her first class. She'd brought as many quarters and single dollar bills with her as she owned, but she definitely didn't have enough to buy a new Diet Coke or bottled water for each class period. Plus, she didn't know much about nutrition, but she figured drinking that many cans of Diet Coke on an otherwise empty stomach would be a poor choice. So Aimee concentrated on making the rest of her Diet Coke last through that first hour, allowing herself to take one sip every seven minutes. By the end of the hour, she had focused so much on when she could drink more pop that she had no idea what they had just learned in class. Her pencil had moved seemingly on its own to take down the notes her teacher wrote on the board, but she remembered not one iota of what it was about. She'd have to make sure she read it all over again that night to make up for her distraction. No biggie. Another excuse to spend time away from watching all of the food her dad and brother seemed to stuff into their mouths constantly.

When lunch finally rolled around, Aimee had already downed two cans of Diet Coke that morning and was halfway through a bottle of water. She still had enough quarters left to buy either one more Diet Coke or one more water and would have to make that beverage last through the afternoon. She decided to challenge her willpower and set a plate of food in front of herself to see if she could resist eating it. Her friends would question her lack of food two days in a row for sure, so she figured she'd better fill up the plate a little more than yesterday.

She saw Jenna in the salad line again. Jenna took several cucumber slices and loaded up on what Aimee thought of as high-calorie foods—croutons, cut-up pieces of fried chicken, cheese, and Thousand Island dressing. Aimee copied her, except she used ranch instead of Thousand Island. There had to be something going on that she didn't understand. How did the girl's stomach manage to look borderline concave if she was actually eating such a large number of calories? Yesterday Aimee had been distracted by Coralee's boy problems and had neglected the study of her anorexic role model's eating habits more than she'd wanted to do. Today she would try to give it a better effort.

She lucked out. Today Jenna sat on the end of the same table where Aimee was sitting, making it much easier to glance down there occasionally to spy. Aimee noticed that the girl spent a large amount of time cutting her cucumbers up into bite-sized pieces and more thoroughly spreading her dressing around on her vegetables, so Aimee repeated those actions. Jenna also seemed to spend much of her lunchtime talking to a couple of her friends, and when she talked, she set down her fork and gestured broadly with her hands. Aimee tried it when her own friends asked her a question. No fork in her hand, no temptation to eat.

When there was a pause in the conversation and her friends were eating, Aimee took a swig of her water rather than taking a bite of salad. Jenna pushed her food around on her plate a lot rather than taking bites, and that action somehow made the food look as though it was getting eaten. Aimee tried that, too. When Jenna *did* take a bite, she ate an extremely dainty piece of cucumber with just a dab of dressing on it. Her bites were so small that they seemed to be the size of what Aimee figured a mouse would consume. On the random occasion when Jenna ate anything other than cucumber, she soon brought her napkin up to her mouth, appearing to wipe her face clear of crumbs. However, Aimee figured she was probably spitting the food out, since she kept her fist tightly closed around the used napkin as if hiding something.

Can I trust myself to taste food and spit it back out? Aimee's mouth watered just thinking about it. Would that be breaking her Diet Coke and water fast? She'd better not try it today—her self-discipline was too weak. Maybe she'd try it tomorrow at lunch.

Her phone buzzed in her pocket, and she pulled it out. It was just a new email, but it reminded her of their principal's strange reply from the previous evening. She opened up the email again and showed her friends.

"Last night I had to email Mr. Owens a couple of questions, and this is what he sent back." Aimee held the phone in front of Meghan first, since she was seated next to her, and then moved it so Coralee could read it on the other side of the table.

Meghan laughed. "What's up with his emojis? Did he type this out when he wasn't even looking at the screen?"

Coralee raised her eyebrows after taking Aimee's phone to get a closer look. "Drunk maybe?"

"Could be. Mrs. Collins said he left early but didn't say why. I just assumed he was sick."

"I think he's drunk. My brother has sent me a text before while he's been at a party, and although it wasn't quite this bad, it was close." Coralee's voice rang with authority.

Meghan's eyes lit up, as if she was calculating with whom she could share this information.

Aimee realized she may have just started a rumor. "You guys *cannot* tell anyone, okay?"

Meghan sighed. "Okay."

Coralee nodded and ate the last bite of her lunch.

In the afternoon Aimee felt even more easily distracted than she had during her morning classes and was so wound up from caffeine that she could barely stay in her seat during geometry. When school let out at 2:30, she had ended her school day with no food, three cans of Diet Coke and one bottle of water. She walked out to her mom's car, shaky but also elated that she had experienced so much success for her article.

Her mom's face was pale and her eyes were closed but squinty, as if she were wincing from pain. Sara had already shifted over to the passenger seat when Aimee arrived at the car. Aimee didn't feel like driving but did not want to explain why. "Mom, is your migraine back?"

"Yeah." Sara sighed softly, keeping her eyes closed and hands clenched tightly together in her lap.

"Sorry, hope it goes away soon," Aimee said equally softly so as not to hurt her mom's already aching head.

They picked up Cody, whom Aimee convinced to keep his voice to just a half-obnoxious volume, and headed back to the house.

"Aimee, will you wash up some lettuce and a couple of other vegetables to put in a salad? I'm going to go lie down for a little while, and I'll get up about 4:30 to put some chicken in the oven."

Aimee really wanted to take a nap herself (the effects of the pop were beginning to wane and now she felt sluggish) but knew her mom needed help. "Okay, I'll do that."

She downed two glasses of water while washing the salad ingredients. She didn't care much for onions but while she was chopping them up found herself tempted to pop a couple of pieces in her mouth. *Just a few more hours, you can do this. Tomorrow you get to EAT!* she rejoiced.

Cody sat on a bar stool while she prepped dinner, cramming Doritos straight from the bag into his mouth and playing on his Nintendo Switch. The buttons were undoubtedly covered with cheesy seasoning from the chips, but he didn't seem to notice. At one point, he uncharacteristically spun the bag around in her direction. "Want one?"

Aimee wanted to take him up on his offer just to encourage his good manners but didn't dare put one of her favorite snacks anywhere close to her fingers. She turned further away from him so she didn't have to look at the shiny red bag of chips. "No, thanks."

She washed the lettuce with renewed vigor, determined to get far away from the tempting scent of the Doritos.

CHAPTER FIVE

Aimee

Aimee almost forgot about her Diet-Coke-and-water plan while she was cutting up the vegetables and especially when Cody started asking her some questions. She was answering the questions, chopping up cucumbers, and as she was transferring the cucumbers from the cutting board to the bowl, she nearly slipped a couple of the pieces that were clinging to the cutting board into her mouth. Her hand was halfway there, mouth open, while nodding and listening to Cody. Suddenly she caught herself and placed the pieces in the bowl. Cody didn't even seem to notice her fumble.

The rest of the night was not so great. Aimee practiced what she had learned from Jenna at lunch and pushed her food around her plate with her fork a lot. She did not, however, actually put any of the food into her mouth to spit into a napkin. She figured that would be too tempting and too easy to accidentally swallow. Nobody said anything about her full plate at the end of the meal. Cody ate two plates of food, her mom was clearly still suffering from a migraine and barely touched any food, and her dad looked really tired. So Aimee was able to scrape her plate of food into the trash can without a second glance from anyone.

After dinner, she tried to concentrate on collecting background information on Josh Trudeau to incorporate into the article about him but was getting headachy from no food and starting to feel nauseous, despite the fact there really wouldn't be anything to throw up even if her body wanted to do so. So she attempted to come up with a solid twelve questions to ask Josh at their coffee meeting the next day and started a half-hearted set of sit-ups. Mom walked in while she was on the floor.

"Wow, exercising? Good job, Aimee." She smiled weakly.

Aimee paused to give her mom a hug. "How are you feeling?"

"Ehhh." Sara shrugged. "A little better. Just wanted to come tell you good night."

"Okay." Aimee eased herself back to the floor. "Good night. See you tomorrow."

"Good luck with your sit-ups. I should do some of those tomorrow if this migraine's gone." Sara headed out the door and closed it softly behind her.

Spurred on by her mother's encouragement, Aimee made it through fifteen more repetitions and then collapsed into bed at a ridiculously early time for her—8:30.

*****

Friday Aimee woke up with a smile on her face. She had survived her Diet-Coke-and-water-only day. Today she was going to get to eat *real food*. She started the morning off with

44

more ab exercises like all the "good" anorexic girls seemed to do on their blogs; she only did twenty-five sit-ups, but at least it was something. (The girls on the blogs did way more, but Aimee's stomach was so new to exercise that twenty-five was all she could take, especially after the ones before bed the previous night.) She figured it was a good effort at least. Not only did she get to eat real food today, but she got to meet Josh Trudeau! She could hardly contain her excitement.

After hurriedly getting dressed and ready for school, she answered her mother's call to breakfast the first time and put a couple of slices of cantaloupe onto her plate along with a spoonful of scrambled eggs and a triangle of ham. She started by biting off a tiny corner of the cantaloupe and savoring the sweet juice. She then drank half of her glass of water and began to cut her ham into small pieces. Her mother sat at the head of the table with a mug of hot tea and a bowlful of fruit. Cody scarfed down his breakfast and a glass of orange juice, playing some Nintendo game again with one hand and transferring his fork from his plate to his mouth with the other. Aimee took a very small bite of scrambled eggs and relished the peppery, cheesy taste of them. All of a sudden she realized she hadn't mentioned her interview with Josh to her parents, and she was going to need a ride to the coffee shop later.

She worked on cutting her melon into microscopic pieces to match the ham. "Mom, I have to do an interview with someone for the school paper at 4:30 this afternoon. I'm supposed to meet him at Biggby Coffee on James Street. Can you give me a ride there?"

Her mom took a sip of tea. "Sure. Who are you meeting?"

"His name is Josh Trudeau. He's from this area but moved to New York after he invented something that turned him into a millionaire. He's only seventeen but he's been a millionaire for almost six months now. He should be pretty interesting to interview."

Sara ate an apple slice. "That sounds like it'll be a good story."

"That's what I thought. I wanted the story originally but Kirsten claimed it. Then she wanted to give the story up because some guy asked her out for tonight, which conflicted with the interview time, and so she offered it to me."

"Cool." Her mother smiled and rose to her feet. "We've got to leave in like five minutes, you guys. Grab more food if you want it. I'm going to start cleaning up."

Aimee took two more bites of cantaloupe and one bite of ham, finished her glass of water, wiped her mouth with her napkin, and hurried to the kitchen to scrape her plate. She was a bit surprised to see much of her mother's bowl of fruit dumped out in the trash.

"Still not feeling well, Mom?" she asked worriedly.

"Oh, I'm actually feeling a lot better, sweetie. Just in a hurry to get you guys to school so you won't be late." Sara smiled and sipped at her peppermint tea again. "I might eat more later, after you guys are at school."

"Okay." Aimee ran upstairs to grab her backpack and took a couple of minutes to check her room for any quarters she might have missed yesterday in her search for vending machine money. Even though she was allowing herself to eat some food today, that Diet Coke trick really had worked well to keep her from feeling so hungry yesterday. It filled her stomach better than just plain water did. It would be nice to be able to have another can or two to help her make it through the day until she could eat supper.

She dug through pants pockets, the bottom of her purse, and quickly ran her hand along the inside of her desk drawers.

She managed to come up with enough quarters for one can and still made it downstairs to the car before her brother.

Sara was sitting in the passenger seat again, encouraging Aimee to work on her driving hours.

The morning at school dragged until lunch. Aimee managed to load up on the salad bar again and actually looked forward to being able to eat part of what was on her plate this time. She had decided that today she would try the spit-the-food into a napkin trick. What the heck. It was her last day of this experiment, after all. She grabbed five napkins from the end of the salad bar in preparation.

Meghan and Coralee regaled her with tales of boys and complaints about test scores for yet another lunch period while Aimee pushed food around on her plate, ate four bites of cucumber with Italian dressing on them, one bite of lettuce with some cheese on it, and a single crouton. She also tried to be sneaky while taking a bite of potato salad, chewing a couple of times, and then carefully "wiping" her mouth so she could spit it out. When no one seemed to notice, she did the same thing two more times. It really wasn't so bad, getting to taste the food and then spitting it out. It was way better than not getting to put anything in her mouth, that was for sure. And it made her look as though she was eating more than she actually was. Perfect. Even though they weren't good habits, Aimee was proud of herself for learning so much about anorexia in such a short time span. She couldn't wait for dinner and hoped her mom was making something amazing.

When school let out, she went home for a bit before the interview and touched up her hair, changed into the same blazer she'd worn for her interview with the principal, and darkened her eye makeup to make herself look more mature. Satisfied with her appearance, she decided to grab something small to snack on before the interview, as she kept experiencing some dizziness and wanted to make sure she didn't pass out at the coffee shop. At this point, she wasn't sure if she was feeling lightheaded due solely to lack of food or to a combination of lack of food and nerves regarding the interview. She honestly hoped Josh wasn't as attractive in person as he was in his pictures online, because if he was, she didn't know if she'd be able to handle the interview in a calm, professional way. For previous articles, Aimee had only ever interviewed boring, ugly adults, never someone her own age. *He's probably a jerk,* she told herself. *Then he won't be as hot.*

At 4:00 her mother drove her the seven miles to Biggby, gave her some money, and told her to call when the interview was over. She was going to shop at some of the clothing stores further down the street while waiting. Aimee had wanted to arrive early so that she could have time to breathe and collect her thoughts before talking to Josh. She bought a chamomile tea and found a small table near the back where she took a seat facing the door. She wondered if Kirsten had told him what she looked like so he would have some idea of who he was meeting. The small restaurant was mostly empty. Two college-aged baristas flirted with each other behind the counter. Only a couple of other tables were occupied—one by a student on a laptop and the second by a pair of sweaty, middle-aged women dressed in yoga pants, T-shirts, and tennis shoes, with bottles of water beside their large plastic cups of iced, sugary coffee topped with mounds of whipped cream.

Sara

Sara had told Aimee she would be shopping, but really

she wasn't sure if she would even leave the parked car. She had been telling her family the truth about feeling ill the past few days, but the headache was only part of the issue. The second part of the problem was that she needed to convince herself to stick with her plan to reset her way of eating. Dave had been spending extra hours at work that week to finish inventory, and his absence had left Sara with more time than usual to spend on her project. Her frequent blog posts that week (twice as often as usual) had really sparked some interest, and her followers had tripled since last Thursday. Oddly enough, she tended to feel like it was more important to be honest with her followers than with Dave. Yesterday she had told her readers that she was going to start the Rainbow Diet today, and she had begun strong at breakfast that morning with her apple slices. She had successfully conquered the Rainbow Diet at least ten times in the past and hadn't expected it to be difficult this time around with so much practice under her belt. An hour after driving her kids to school, though, the hunger pangs and cravings hit. She had been looking through recipes online, trying to decide what to make for dinner, and the sight of a rogue ice cream sundae (Where did that come from, anyway? She had searched for chicken dishes.) pushed her over the edge. There was no ice cream in the house, but she had eaten almost an entire bag of chocolate chips in the course of thirty minutes. Following that disaster, she'd sobbed, disgusted with herself for fifteen minutes before searching out her laxatives. It was okay—she could make things right again.

But *Dave*!

Dave must have been busy cleaning while she was napping away her headaches that week because her shoebox in the hall closet was empty. She sunk onto her hands and knees, reaching into the dark depths of the closet behind the shoes and floor-length coats, just in case a miracle had happened and the pills had fallen to the back. Nothing remained except a four-year-old receipt. Treasure walked up and nuzzled his way underneath her searching hands until she stopped hunting for the laxatives and started petting him. Dave had trashed her stash, and she didn't think she had the physical or emotional energy to make a trip to the store at the moment. All of the love and support her followers had offered once she'd announced she was beginning the Rainbow Diet would turn to disappointment when she shared about the binge disaster. She hadn't even lasted one day on the week-long diet. Sara dreaded her nightly weigh-in.

The longer she sat in the car, worrying about her weigh-in and whether her sugary choice that day would turn away followers when she confessed later, Sara realized that at least shopping would burn a few calories. Now that the hundreds of chocolatey calories had kicked in, she was feeling more energetic and could perhaps push herself to walk around a clothing store a few times while waiting for Aimee's call. Today was a loss, but she would restart her Rainbow Diet the next day.

Aimee

Aimee sipped her tea, grasping the mug with both hands to stop them from trembling. She was really feeling like she needed to eat more, but she sucked in slow, deep breaths and managed to regain control of her hands. The warmth of the mug helped.

At 4:26, while Aimee was studying over her interview questions and doodling in the corner of one of the pages, the bell above the door rang. She jerked her head up but was disappointed to see a tall, young couple enter the shop rather than the subject of her interview. She returned to drawing stars in the corner of her first page and glanced at her phone to see if she'd gotten any new texts or emails.

"Excuse me."

Aimee jumped and looked up to see Josh Trudeau standing in front of her table. He was just as handsome as his pictures but much shorter than she'd expected. He must have walked in behind the couple.

"I'm Josh. Are you Kirsten?"

Aimee shook her head and rose quickly, grabbing the table to steady herself. "I'm Aimee, actually. Kirsten was supposed to call you and let you know I would be doing the interview instead of her. Something came up." She was about to ramble on that Kirsten was a bit of a flake and had irresponsibly chosen a date with someone over meeting with Josh but caught herself just in time.

She stuck out her hand to shake Josh's. He stood just two inches taller than she, which put him at a solid five foot six. "Sorry about the confusion. If I'd known she didn't call you, I would've called you myself."

"Oh, no problem." Josh smiled graciously and returned her handshake. "I'm going to go grab something to drink before we start the interview. Would you like me to get you anything?"

"I'm fine, thanks." She gestured to her cup of tea on the table.

"Okay." He smiled again, and Aimee nearly swooned. Short or not, he was just as hot as his pictures online.

She took her seat at the table again and waited for Josh to purchase a cappuccino and a bagel. As she watched him, she suddenly wondered if it would have been proper etiquette for her to have offered to buy him something. After all, she was the one who had invited him here (or rather, Kirsten). *Too late now.*

He returned to the table and began spreading cream cheese onto his bagel. The scent of fresh bread filled Aimee's nose. Her mouth watered, but she simply took another sip of her tea. "So, what's your first question?" he asked.

"Well…" She glanced down at her list. "I know you invented a computer game, Tyrannosaurus Scoop. I saw several descriptions of it online, but I'd like to hear about it from you, in your own words."

He talked for several minutes, using excited, grandiose hand gestures to amplify the story, and Aimee found herself genuinely interested in his game, despite the fact that she had virtually no experience in gaming.

"How did you decide to create Tyrannosaurus Scoop?"

"My mom had cancer three years ago, and my grandparents' way of helping our family was keeping mine and my brother's minds off of the issue by buying us new video games regularly. We would each take turns sitting with my mom while she received her chemo treatments, but she would usually fall asleep or not feel up to talking while there. So I always took my laptop when it was my turn. One day while I was there with her, I decided to try creating my own video game, incorporating similar ideas from my favorite video games and eliminating things I didn't like about those same video games. I really enjoyed working on it, and eventually I was spending all of my free time creating this game. When I had a test version of it ready to go, my younger brother tried it and loved Tyrannosaurus Scoop. At that point, my mom was done with her cancer treatments, and our family was able to spend more time together. I showed the game to my parents, and my dad helped me research to figure out how to turn the game into a source of income. Once the game was finally available for others to buy a few months ago, I decided to donate a portion of the profits to help those with cancer pay for their medical bills."

"That is…amazing," Aimee muttered, awestruck at the brilliance and compassion of this teenager. She finished writing out her notes before asking him the next question.

Forty minutes passed while Josh became the most interesting interview subject she had ever spent time with. He even downloaded a sample copy of Tyrannosaurus Scoop onto her phone to try at home. She filled pages and pages with notes and began to wonder how she was going to condense everything into a 500-word article for the school newspaper. Maybe Mrs. Bennett would allow her to expand it by at least a couple hundred more words.

They had finished their drinks and Josh his bagel when he stretched and asked, "Do you like Maroon 5? I have tickets to their concert tonight, and my friend backed out on me. Would you like to go with me?"

Aimee's eyes widened in disbelief. "Maroon 5 is one of my favorites. I can't believe you like them, too! None of my friends like them. I would love to go! Are you sure you want me to go with you, though?"

"Of course—I wouldn't have asked if I didn't mean it." He winked.

Aimee grinned. "I just have to make sure it's okay with my parents."

She called her mom, who acted hesitant about Aimee taking off to a concert with a guy she had just met. "I think I'll come meet him first."

"Mom!" Aimee felt her cheeks reddening, even though Josh couldn't hear what her mother had just said. "Please? Just let me do this? What if I text you every couple of hours to let you know I'm all right?"

Sara sighed. "Okay, sweetie, but be careful. Are you guys getting dinner, too?"

"I don't know, we'll see." Dinner! Tonight was supposed to be the night Aimee was allowed to return to eating normal, full meals. Plus, she was supposed to work on her article about Josh that evening.

I'll just stay up when I get home tonight and work on it. No big deal.

As for dinner, even if Josh did take her out for a meal, Aimee didn't know if she could eat due to nervousness at his proximity. After hearing his story she had gained admiration and respect for him, and those feelings only increased her attraction to him.

She felt slightly glad that she had dieted the past few days. Somehow, it caused her to feel more self-controlled and made her think that her extra little bit of thinness probably made her more attractive in Josh's eyes.

After ending the call with her mother, she walked back over to the table, where Josh was playing on his phone. "What time is the concert?"

"Opening band starts at 6:30. The concert's in Grand Rapids, so we'd better get going." He stood up.

"Okay." No mention of dinner. Just as well, she probably wouldn't have been able to eat much, anyway.

On the ride to Grand Rapids, Josh talked more about his family and his life in New York. "I really miss it here, though," he commented. "We had a house on twelve acres of land when we lived here, and the open space was so nice. My brother and

I used to ride around on four-wheelers all the time and explore in the woods. Everything's so crowded in New York. It's hard to get away by yourself and get some peace and quiet."

Aimee wished she had something awesome to contribute to the conversation but simply nodded. She'd lived in the same house in a subdivision her whole life. She'd never even vacationed to New York City. "So... how long are you in Michigan for this time?"

"Just a week. We're visiting my grandparents." He flicked on the turn signal, and they pulled into the parking ramp for Van Andel Arena.

"Cool." She stuck her sweaty hands, palm-up, beneath her thighs. At least once the concert started, she wouldn't be expected to be a great conversationalist.

He asked her questions about school and the school newspaper. She almost told him about her anorexic experiment but caught herself. Even though she had been dieting simply for the sake of an article, she didn't want him to think she was a nutcase. She couldn't believe Kirsten had given up the interview for a date with Trey. They were probably just going to go to some stupid guy movie or something, but Aimee got to go to a Maroon 5 concert for *free* with Josh, the seventeen-year-old millionaire. She could just picture Kirsten's face when she told her Monday morning. *Sometimes it pays to be the responsible, straight-A student,* she told herself smugly.

When they finally found their seats, Aimee was uneasy once she realized just how far up in the arena they would be sitting. The lack of food combined with extreme height severely messed with her head. She sat down quickly, afraid she was going to fall over the seats below them. *I really should have eaten at the coffee shop.*

They had enjoyed the first couple of songs from the

opening band and were in between songs when Josh leaned over and asked if she'd like something to drink.

"Sure, how about a Coke?" she suggested, wishing he'd offer food instead but not wanting to sound rude by asking. She secretly hoped he'd pick up something to snack on anyway. But at the very least, she got to drink *real* Coke this time, not diet crap. She was excited.

When he returned from the concession stands, he handed her a large cup. "They were out of normal Coke, so I got you diet. I hope that's okay. And just to clarify, you don't look like you need to drink Diet Coke or anything," he stammered. "You're tiny."

Aimee laughed and accepted the drink. "No worries. Thanks, Josh." She took a long drag of it through the straw. *Hello, old friend.* Josh had called her "tiny"! She beamed inside.

He held a bottle of water for himself, and…no food. He probably wasn't hungry—he'd eaten a bagel at Biggby.

Aimee focused on the concert while the Diet Coke filled her stomach. It took about half an hour for the stage crew to set up in preparation for Adam Levine, and Josh told her about his typical day-to-day life in New York while they waited.

"So, do you go to school?" Aimee asked. If she had become a millionaire at age seventeen, she probably would have dropped out of school. If her parents let her.

"I do. When we first moved to New York, it was almost the end of the school year, so my parents home-schooled me for the remaining two months. I hated it—as much as I love my mom, we definitely needed a break from each other, and I missed having other people my age around. So, this fall I entered a public high school in New York. No one there knows anything about my video game yet and I'm working at keeping it that way, so it's perfect."

"Seriously? No one knows who you are?"

"Look at it this way…had you heard of me before you were asked to write an article about me?"

She straightened up. "Well, I kind of remember you from our elementary school, but…"

"Had you heard of Tyrannosaurus Scoop?"

She blushed. "I, uh, well, I don't really game, but, uh, I'm sure I would have heard of you if I did more of that sort of thing."

"See? It's nothing to be embarrassed about. I've been interviewed a few times because I am so young and because of the game itself, but the truth of the matter is, I became a millionaire based on how much a company offered me to buy my idea. I get a small cut of the profit from each one sold, but for right now, few people know who created it. I drive a used car I bought for $3,000 when I go to and from school, which is pretty much in line with what my classmates drive. No one has any idea, and I like it that way. It's helped me to make some friends who like me for me, not for my money."

Aimee nodded. He was so smart for only being seventeen. "Hey, do you mind if I put some of this other information you're telling me in my article? If you want me to stick to what we talked about at the coffee shop, I will, but some of this other information will really help to round out the article."

"Sure, that's fine," he agreed, sobering up and looking slightly sad.

Aimee thought through what she had said and wondered what could possibly have made him sad. "Is something wrong, Josh?"

"No, I just…for a minute, I forgot that this meeting was about the article." He pursed his lips.

Aimee scrambled for what to say next. "The coffee shop

meeting was, but this concert really isn't. You just have a lot of interesting things to say, and I want to share that information with others. I'm having a lot of fun with you. Thank you for inviting me!"

He smiled, and fortunately the opening chords of "This Love" began, relieving Aimee from having to justify her words further.

While she sang along with Adam, Aimee analyzed Josh's earlier hurt expression and what he had said. Was he viewing this concert as a date? Had he been offended because he thought she had only agreed to the concert as a means of learning more about his lifestyle for her newspaper article? She enjoyed the idea of thinking of the concert as a date but at the same time didn't know how a guy like Josh could possibly be attracted to her. She was just a normal, fifteen-year-old middle-class teenager who hadn't invented anything. At the same time, he had asked her to go to the concert (and had paid for the tickets), he had driven her to Van Andel, and he had bought her a drink.

When she put the facts together that way, it sure seemed like a date, although that made her look a little desperate for agreeing to go out with him at the last minute. It also made her wonder about Josh's expectations regarding the evening. Maybe her mom had been right to be concerned—she shouldn't be out alone with some guy she'd just met a couple of hours ago. She glanced over at him and smiled when she saw him singing along at the top of his lungs, enjoying every second of the concert. *So cute.*

Suddenly she felt more self-conscious than she had all evening and smoothed a hand down the wrinkles in the front of her blazer. The mini rush of adrenaline caused the lightheadedness she'd experienced earlier to return, and Aimee gripped the top of the seat in front of her. She forced herself to focus on the stage rather than the steep drop to the floor below. If only she could sit for a minute, she'd probably be fine. But if she sat, Josh would ask her what was wrong, and then he'd think she was crazy for not eating.

A miracle occurred at the end of the song when Josh leaned over to say he was going out for a minute to make a call. She watched his back as he headed down the stairs, and then she gratefully sank into her seat and finished her Diet Coke. She pulled out her phone, remembering that she'd promised her mom a text every couple of hours.

Hey Mom, just wanted to let you know I'm okay. We're still at the concert, probably be home in an hour or two.

She watched her phone until Josh returned, but there was no response from her mother.

Her mouth salivated when she honed in on the plastic carton of nachos in his strong hand. She'd wanted nachos since the first day of her experiment. Aimee certainly didn't know Josh well enough to just reach over and take one, but it was all she could do to keep her empty right hand to herself. Her left hand clutched her cell phone, preventing it from reaching out and snatching up the food like a starving lion in Africa.

Josh dipped a chip into the artificially yellow cheese and brought it up to his mouth. After chewing, he said the magic words. "Would you like one?"

Aimee smiled and restrained herself from sticking her whole face into the snack. "Sure, thanks." She could feel her hand trembling, both from excitement at the prospect of food and from blood sugar problems due to restriction, and she managed to gracefully take just one chip and daintily dip it into the cheese, tapping it along the edge of the molded plastic carton to prevent it from dripping onto the floor (or even worse, onto Josh's leg!) in between the carton and her mouth.

She barely prevented herself from cramming the entire chip into her mouth at once. As soon as she'd chewed and swallowed, she wanted to reach for another but figured she'd better be polite and wait for another invitation for a chip. He ate a couple more and then held the carton out for her again. She accepted, and so the dance continued. He would eat two or three, offer her the container, and she would eat another. By the time she'd downed six or seven, she felt like she might get sick if she ate anymore. Nachos were not exactly easy on one's stomach to begin with, let alone eaten on a stomach that had basically remained empty for three days. So she regretfully declined more chips, grateful she had been able to enjoy a few but also disappointed in the state of her stomach.

It was almost 11:00 when the concert ended, and Aimee dreaded the walk back down the steep stairs to the ground floor. She was feeling less dizzy but still slightly off-balance, and her stomach was feeling worse than it had before she'd eaten. She should have been smart and held off on eating until she got home, where she could have eased back into the land of food with some carrots or something.

Josh started down the treacherous stairs first, and Aimee followed closely behind, concerned about losing him in the crowded chaos. They were both so short—it would be easy to get separated from each other. She clung tightly to the railing on the cement steps and yelped when she stumbled. Her left hand, the one not busy gripping the rail, instinctively reached out and grabbed Josh's shoulder to steady herself.

He didn't falter at all but instead turned and looked up at

her. "Are you okay? Here." He held out his hand for her to take.

Aimee blushed again, unsure what to do. She was embarrassed for latching onto him but also confused by the offer of his hand. Was it simply a chivalrous gesture to keep her from falling, or was it meant to be partly a romantic gesture? She wasn't sure but was still scared of plummeting to her death, so she took his hand. The crowd pressed in around the two of them, but Aimee felt safe with her hand nestled in Josh's.

He continued to hold onto her hand at the bottom of the stairs, although his grip loosened up a little. She secretly reveled in the warmth of his hand, and the longer the attachment continued, the more she wondered if he had meant it romantically. There was still the concern that they could lose each other in the crowd, though, so she rationalized that was probably why he continued to hang onto her.

They finally reached a place where the crowd was beginning to thin as the two stepped out of the building and into the cool night air. Josh let go of her hand.

Aimee sighed softly, her hand longing to fold back into his.

"So what did you think of the concert?" he asked.

"It was fantastic!" She recounted her two favorite parts. "Thank you so much for letting me come with you."

"My pleasure," he said, and she glanced from the sidewalk in front of her to meet his eyes.

I wish I could kiss him right now flashed through her mind. With that thought, the blush on her face returned.

He cleared his throat. "You know what? I think we might be walking away from the car at the moment."

She looked all around and had no idea where she was.

"You might be right."

They stopped and turned, and Josh pointed to their left. "I think the parking garage is that way."

They changed direction, and Aimee wrapped her arms around herself as they walked. A light snow was falling, and her jacket was starting to feel too thin. She dug her hands in her pockets to see if there was a pair of gloves inside but had no success. Before she knew it, Josh had handed her a pair of leather gloves.

"Here, these were in my coat pocket if you want to wear them."

"Thank you," she said gratefully, tucking her hands into his gloves.

"I think we're almost there."

On the hour-long ride back to Aimee's house, they listened to the radio and didn't talk much. "If I give you my address in New York, will you mail me a copy of the paper with your article in it when it comes out?" Josh asked her at one point.

"Yes, of course," she agreed. Now there was even more pressure to write the article well so that he would be satisfied by how she portrayed his life. Aimee peeked at the clock on the dash and grimaced at the fact that it was midnight already. Should she sleep when she got home and get up early to write the article or just stay up all night and work on it? *Ugghhhh*. This was why she didn't usually have much of a social life—it was difficult to do well on her schoolwork and keep her personal life organized when she spent too much time with friends.

When they arrived at her house, Aimee yawned, gathered up her purse and the notebook she had used to interview Josh, and reached for the door handle. "Thank you so much for everything, Josh; I appreciate that you let me interview you. I had a great time at the concert!"

"Thanks for going with me—you're pretty fun to hang out with." He grinned. "Good luck with the article. You have my phone number, right? Let me know if you need anything else while you're writing it."

"Thanks." She suddenly remembered the leather gloves on her hands and removed them. It stunk that she wouldn't be able to see him again. Even if there was nothing romantic about their relationship, it would have been fun to have Josh as a friend. It didn't matter whether he had money or not—he was nice and seemed more mature than many of the other teenagers she knew. "I hope the rest of your time in Michigan is fun."

He smiled. "Well, even if it isn't, I had a blast tonight."

She grinned and opened the door. "Bye, Josh."

"Bye, Aimee."

He didn't pull out of the driveway until she was safely inside her house. She set her purse and notebook on the bench in the entryway and bent down to remove her shoes. A light was glowing from her parents' office down the hall.

She peeked into the room. Her mom looked like she was reading a blog or something.

"Hey, Mom."

"Aimee!" Her mother quickly minimized the page she was reading. "I only heard from you once—I was concerned."

"Oh, sorry. I had a really good time, though," Aimee said. "I forgot to text you again."

Her mom nodded. "I didn't expect you home this late. I know I didn't give you a curfew, but this really is kind of late. Next time I want to know how long you're planning to be gone."

"Okay. I have to go work on an article—it's due tomorrow afternoon," Aimee said, backing out of the room.

"Did your interview go okay?"

"It did. I learned a lot of interesting things about Josh. I think this is going to be a good article."

"Great."

"I'll see you in the morning." Aimee headed upstairs to her room and turned her laptop on to get right to work. She had typed a couple of opening sentences when she realized that Josh had never given her his address so that she could send him a copy of the paper.

Aimee deleted emails while debating whether to call or text him about the address thing. He didn't have her phone number, so he couldn't call her. Would it be too forward for her to call him? If she couldn't send him the paper, she would be less nervous about writing the article. Even though he was undoubtedly still awake right now, she felt awkward calling so late at night. She'd wait until tomorrow so that she could think about the situation some more and decide the best course of action.

CHAPTER SIX

Sara

Sara was unable to sleep knowing that Aimee hadn't arrived home yet, so she had gone on the computer after Dave conked out for the night. She had been immersed in working on her blog for over an hour when Aimee managed to silently slip in the house. It had been difficult to admit to her followers that she'd sabotaged her diet, but already she was so glad that she had been honest. The comments had come pouring in just minutes after posting, with many people telling her not to give up. One person offered to start the diet with her in the morning and asked if she could have Sara's email address so they could keep each other accountable. She also asked for a refresher on what the Rainbow Diet was so that she could be sure she was doing it correctly. Sara scrolled through some old posts of her own and found one that described the Rainbow Diet. Monday was white food, Tuesday was yellow food, Wednesday was a fast, Thursday was orange food, and so on and so forth. All foods eaten those days were small amounts of fruit and vegetables. She gave the commenter the link to the old post and, after some hesitation, provided her email address. It would be nice to have an accountability partner.

After she was certain Aimee had gone upstairs, Sara refreshed her page and checked for new comments. There was only one from someone by the name of Ana's Servant:

Do you personally know anyone who has died from anorexia? I love all of your tips!

Sara looked at the clock—12:30 a.m. She didn't want to deal with this question tonight. She'd think about whether to answer or ignore and just go to sleep for now.

Aimee

Aimee forgot about eating and stayed up until 3 a.m. working on her article about Josh. She slept for four hours and then got up to see if she could figure out how to play the copy of Tyrannosaurus Scoop that Josh had given her. She joined Cody in the living room, where he was watching some sports movie.

Half an hour later, she could barely get two minutes into the game without all of the cavemen dying. Whenever her dinosaur moved toward them, flailing an umbrella in his tiny arms, the men ran off a cliff. How on earth was he supposed to scoop anything up with those short arms? After her first few sighs of frustration, Cody had sat down next to her on the couch, studying the game carefully and crunching on a bowl of cereal.

"I'll show you what to do." His bowl clattered onto the

coffee table as he grabbed her phone and took over.

Aimee started to protest but ended up just watching her little brother play. As the dinosaur wandered out onto the screen yet again wearing a top hat, Cody quickly began pressing all sorts of buttons and was able to scoop up several fleeing cavemen with the inside of the umbrella on his first try. She assumed the dinosaur was going to eat the cavemen, but Cody seemed to innately know that the dinosaur needed to carry the men safely back to their homes. Several times, the dinosaur fought off other monsters along the way. She laughed at the Tyrannosaurus Rex's victory dance each time he defeated a monster. Cody finished level one and smugly passed the phone back to his sister. "I have to go change for soccer."

Aimee returned to her room and spent another two hours perfecting her assignment (which now included details of the game) before emailing it off to Mrs. Bennett just before 10:30. It had turned out to be nearly one thousand words. She sent both a long version and a short version to Mrs. Bennett but preferred the longer one herself. She took a break from writing to jump in the shower and grab some breakfast.

When she stripped in front of the bathroom mirror, Aimee noticed just how thin her stomach looked, compared to how it had looked at the beginning of the week. It was amazing what a few days of dieting could do. Yesterday she had enjoyed how loose her jeans were. As much as she hated feeling like she could pass out, she was also enjoying feeling thinner than normal. Just out of curiosity, she stepped on the scale. With just three days of dieting, she had already lost three pounds! Aimee couldn't help but smile.

Her mom never cooked breakfast for everybody on the weekends, so Aimee was on her own for food after getting cleaned up. She decided to try to pick something healthy—

although she was eating again, she wanted to use this extreme diet as a reset for a healthier lifestyle. The nachos from last night had not felt like such a good idea once they were in her stomach, so she figured she should probably pick something easier to digest this time around.

She selected an apple from the refrigerator and headed back to her room. Her mom's voice carried up the stairs. "Aimee, we're headed out for Cody's game. We won't be home for lunch, but there are leftovers from yesterday's dinner if you want to heat something up."

"All right. Thanks, Mom." She plopped in front of her computer and chewed the apple as she thought of the best way to start her anorexia article. Technically she only needed to create an outline for now, but she was eager to write the actual article. She flipped through the pages of research she had printed out a couple of days earlier and decided to start with statistics in the beginning of her article.

After a couple of paragraphs of facts, Aimee launched into the story of her own experiment and teetered between being openly honest and concealing some of what she'd gone through the past few days. She didn't want to make Mrs. Bennett look bad—the woman still didn't even know what topic Aimee had selected for her article, so nothing was her fault. But after all, at several points Aimee had felt as though she might pass out, and if she had actually fainted while driving or something, that could've been…well, fatal. The last thing she wanted to do was make Mrs. Bennett get in trouble for allowing a student to be in a dangerous situation. However, if Aimee omitted how she felt while extreme dieting, it seemed like she was leaving out an important chunk of the article. She wrote about how she'd hidden her food avoidance from others by filling her plate and pushing the food around a lot and by spitting bites out into napkins. She also wrote about how she'd sustained herself entirely on Diet Coke and water one day. The more she thought about it, the more she was proud of herself for the self-discipline she'd exercised the past few days when it came to food. She wrote about what she'd learned regarding calorie counting and how an entire blog community existed to provide support for those with eating disorders. As she wrapped up the article, she grew concerned that her writing glorified anorexia too much and perhaps was teaching other people how to be anorexic. As she labored over what to edit and continued to wrestle with including the feeling of impending blackouts, she checked her email. Mrs. Bennett had emailed her back and commented that she *loved* the long version of the article about Josh. Mrs. Bennett wanted to put Josh's article on the front page, *above the fold*. Prime location.

This was Aimee's first time for such an important space in the paper—usually only seniors had their articles printed on the front page. Squealing with excitement, she quickly wrote Mrs. Bennett back to thank her.

Now would probably be a good time to take a break from her anorexia article. She did feel as though she had a high standard to live up to with her future submitted articles now that she was receiving above-the-fold attention, but after all, the only thing she owed Mrs. Bennett was an outline in a week and a half. Aimee certainly had plenty of time to work.

She logged onto Twitter. There was a message from Josh from 9:00 that morning, and he was now following her.

Hi Aimee, I forgot to give you my address last night. I put it below for you. I had a great time with you. Good luck with your article!

She beamed and followed him back. So things hadn't just been on her end; Josh really did enjoy spending time with her. He'd told her that last night, but seeing it in writing made it a bigger deal. She hoped she'd be able to see him again before he returned to New York but tried not to get her hopes up too much. He would be busy visiting family and hanging out with people who had been his friends much longer than she had been. He wouldn't have time for her.

When she responded to Josh and told him that her teacher had liked the article so much that it was going to be on the front page, she was surprised that he messaged her back immediately.

That's fantastic, Aimee! We should go celebrate.

Her wish was coming true! She paused before typing anything back. She wasn't sure if she could classify last night's concert as a date or not (especially if it was true that his friend had backed out last-minute and he had an extra concert ticket); but if they hung out again, she was going to interpret it as a date this time. That put a lot of pressure on her. *Going on a date with a millionaire when I've never even had a boyfriend before?*

Her parents would be stuck at Cody's game all day—there was some kind of tournament or something, so she'd be on her own until supper. Her fingers hovered above the keyboard as she debated what to say.

I would be up for that.

She fought herself from clarifying whether he meant today or not. *Calm down. Let him give you the details.*

Great! Do you want to grab a late lunch today? I could pick you up at 1:30.

It was 11:45 now. Didn't it break all of the dating rules if she agreed on such short notice? But then again, did it change the rules if someone was only in town for a week? She wasn't really looking forward to staying home by herself all day now that her article was finished, and she wasn't old enough to drive anywhere on her own.

Sure. Do you remember how to get to my house?

I think so. I'll call you if I get lost. What's your number?

She sucked in a quick breath. He was asking for her phone number? Kirsten really had missed out on all the fun by going on a date with dumb Trey.

Aimee gave him her cell number and quickly excused herself from chatting with a brief,

See you in a little bit.

She needed time to figure out what to wear and whether she should tell her parents where she was headed. She had been lucky that her mom had been the one she'd talked to yesterday; if it had been her dad, he probably would've said no to the concert in the first place and definitely would have vetoed a repeat date when she'd come in so late last night. Should she text them to let them know now or just leave a note on the kitchen counter so that if they came home early, they would know where she was?

She decided on the note option—if she arrived back home before they did, Aimee could throw the note away and wouldn't even have to tell them she'd left the house if she didn't want to. This way she would be covered if they came home early and she was missing. She would look at least semi-responsible for telling them where she was going.

She scribbled out a brief message on a large Post-it:

I went to lunch with Josh. Be back soon.

She stuck the bright pink paper to the counter where they would be sure to see it.

Hmmmm, I'd better take some money just in case it's not a date and I end up having to pay for myself. She dug through her purse upstairs but only had a couple of dollars left from what her mom had given her for the coffee shop. She had spent all of her allowance on the stupid vending machine. Aimee wondered if her parents had any money in their dresser drawers that she could maybe borrow and pay back later, if she left that information on the note, too. She walked down the hall to their bedroom and started in her dad's top dresser drawer. No money. She eyed the change jar on top of his dresser, which undoubtedly contained enough coins to cover lunch, but she didn't want to look poverty-stricken in front of Josh. She moved down to the second drawer and was lifting up pairs of pants when she saw a brightly-colored flyer tucked in between the folded jeans. She picked up the tri-folded brochure and was startled when she noticed it was an advertisement for an eating disorder clinic. Did her parents think something was really wrong with her? She'd avoided food for less than a week—how had her parents noticed it that quickly but hadn't said anything to her? She'd need to convince them that her eating habits were healthy and do so in a hurry, too, before they shipped her off to some ward for insane people.

Next to the brochure, she found an envelope with $100 in it and grabbed a twenty, then wrote on the note that she'd borrowed the money. *Well, wait, if they know I saw the envelope, they'll know I saw the brochure, too.* Maybe she'd just borrow the money and then pay it back without telling her parents. She probably wasn't going to have to use the cash, anyway. Josh would probably (hopefully) pay for her and then she could put the money back today, and no one would even notice it was gone.

Aimee ripped up the note and re-wrote her original message then left it on the kitchen counter. When the doorbell rang, announcing that Josh had arrived, she drew in a deep, excited breath and hurried to the front door to greet him.

CHAPTER SEVEN

Aimee

Aimee didn't know what to expect but was glad that Josh just wanted to eat at TGI Fridays. As much as it would have been a fun experience to eat somewhere fancier, she was glad to get to spend time at a casual, familiar place with him (especially since she still was unsure whether it was a date and didn't know if she was going to have to pay for her own food).

He held the door to the restaurant open for her, and they stood around awkwardly for a few minutes in the lobby while waiting for an available table. In the car, they'd spent the drive talking about all the highlights from last night's concert, but now Aimee felt as though she was out of things to discuss.

"So…what are you and your family going to do tonight?" she finally asked.

"Oh, we were supposed to go to my grandparents' house to celebrate my grandma's birthday, but my grandma called this morning and said she wasn't feeling well. She asked if we could raincheck it until tomorrow night, so now tonight is pretty open."

Aimee nodded. "Well, I hope she feels better soon."

"Thanks." He glanced at the screen on his phone and then over at her with an unexpected timid look on his face. "Would you like to hang out with some of my friends and me tonight? Scott just texted me, and a group of people are getting together to play video games and stuff."

Video games? Ughhh. It sounded really boring, but Aimee had a lot of questions regarding the fact that Josh had just invited her. Why did he want to hang out with her so much? Did he like her as more than a friend? For a moment she'd wondered if maybe he just didn't have many friends in Michigan, which seemed unlikely because he was such a nice person, but now he'd just invited her to hang out with *other people* who were his friends. Did he like her enough that he wanted her to meet his friends and get their opinions on her later?

"I, uh…I'll have to ask my parents if it's okay. I'll let you know as soon as I can." There. That didn't sound too eager but still interested. She didn't want to play video games, and in fact knew she would probably embarrass herself if she even tried to play video games after this morning's Tyrannosaurus Scoop disaster, but it would be nice to hang out with Josh again. *What a weird, unexpected weekend.* Before yesterday, she had no prospects for dates and was consumed with her position at the school newspaper, and now she was maybe on her way to having a real boyfriend.

"Oh, okay." He texted a response to his friend, and the hostess showed them to their table.

Even as Aimee's stomach rumbled, she found herself mentally adding up calories of all of the items she would normally not think twice about ordering. As she flipped through laminated pages, she ended up deciding a Caesar salad with chicken was her best bet.

Josh ordered one of the sandwiches and an appetizer of mozzarella sticks. The waitress set the appetizer in the middle of the table just a few minutes later, and Josh motioned for Aimee to dig in. "Help yourself."

"No, they're yours. I'm fine." Aimee batted at the air with her hand to reassure him that the mozzarella sticks weren't important to her.

"I ordered them to share," he insisted, pushing the plate a little closer to her.

She smiled. "Well, maybe just one." She snatched one off the plate and dipped it in the container of marinara sauce. As soon as the red sauce hit her tongue, she immediately felt guilty but wasn't sure why.

You're allowed to eat now, silly. It was just one mozzarella stick, after all. It was certainly unhealthy, all fried and cheesy, and probably like 100 calories in one stick, but…well…

I don't know if I can eat this.

The small bite lingered in her mouth, tucked in one cheek, as she watched Josh dip his own mozzarella stick into the sauce and enthusiastically eat half of the stick in one bite. Aimee forced herself to chew some more, but the more liquefied the bite got, the more she thought about how unhealthy mozzarella sticks were and how she really shouldn't eat even one. *Trying to start healthy habits, remember?* She glanced over at her napkin, hastily rolled around her silverware. She swallowed the bite slowly, setting the remainder of the stick on her tiny appetizer plate and unrolling her silverware. If she only took one bite and didn't eat the rest, Josh would ask her what was wrong. But maybe, *maybe*, she could do the napkin trick. Not for the sake of cutting calories, but because with all of the research she had done on anorexia and dieting and nutrition, the more she realized just how bad fried foods were for one's body. *I don't have an eating disorder. I may have acted like I had one the past few days, but I don't really. I merely don't want to eat something unhealthy.*

The rest of the mozzarella stick was carefully chewed, not swallowed, and surreptitiously deposited into her napkin.

When Josh tried to get her to eat another one, she begged off, claiming she hadn't been that hungry to begin with and wanted to save room for her meal. He seemed to accept that reason.

The chicken smelled wonderful when it arrived at the table. Aimee eyed the plate, excited that overall, its contents looked fairly healthy. As she cut the chicken into bite-sized pieces, she carefully scraped off as much dressing as she could and, almost without thinking, pushed some of the croutons to the side as well. Josh had already eaten a quarter of his sandwich by the time she finally took a bite.

As Josh talked, she savored the taste of the grilled meat. While the waitress refilled her empty glass with water a few minutes after serving their entrees, Aimee realized all of a sudden that she was full. It was probably just because of starving herself the past few days or maybe because of drinking so much water, but she genuinely felt like she'd eaten a lot of food already. She pushed a couple more bites of lettuce onto her fork for one final bite, but Josh asked her a question before the fork made it to her mouth. By the time she finished answering, she wondered what she was doing. After all, if she was full, she shouldn't keep eating. That seemed like the healthy choice. So she set her fork back down and wiped her mouth with her napkin, leaning back in the booth and watching Josh enthusiastically finish his own meal. Half of the salad sat untouched on her plate.

"So…have you heard back from your parents yet about tonight?"

Aimee glanced at her phone. Her dad had texted her that it was fine, surprisingly. "Uh, yes. They're okay with it."

"Cool." He grinned. "We can head over there now, if you want."

"Oh, I didn't realize we were going over so soon," she responded, glancing at the time on her phone again. She had sort of been hoping for a chance to take a nap first. Last night was catching up with her.

"Yeah, Scott said he didn't care what time we came over."

"Okay, then."

"We can stay longer if you want to eat more," he said, gesturing to her plate.

"I'm full, but thank you."

"You hardly ate anything!"

"I really am full," she tried to convince him. Even though she'd eaten probably fewer than 300 calories, it was more than she'd consumed in a single meal the past few days. The thought of shoving another few bites of food into her stomach made her feel sick. She placed her balled-up napkin, containing the bites of mozzarella stick, on top of her messy plate. There, now she wouldn't be tempted to consider eating more.

"Okay," he said unconvincingly, and as if the waitress had been waiting for Aimee to signal that she was done, she swooped in and set the check on the table. Aimee didn't even have a chance to wonder if she was supposed to pay for her own meal. Josh snatched up the check and pulled out his debit card so fast that she barely had time to think.

She blushed as soon as she realized what that gesture meant. It was a date.

"Thanks for the meal, Josh." She tucked her hair behind her ear and hoped and prayed that she didn't have any food on her face.

"Well, we had to celebrate your article! That's cool you'll be on the front page." He grinned.

If this was a date, and if last night had been kind of a date too, once he headed back to New York, what did this whole situation mean? Aimee was attracted to him, and what she'd seen of his personality so far she liked, but was there honestly even a chance that something between a middle-class fifteen-year-old and a genius millionaire seventeen-year-old could last? The odds were not good. She would see how this video game party went tonight.

"Ready to head over to Scott's?"

"Sure."

Sara

Sara knew something was up as soon as David told Aimee she could hang out with her new guy friend that evening. Dave hadn't even met the boy yet, and she'd expected him to be much more protective and cautious. And then when he'd offered to drop Cody and his friends off at a movie that night, she grew even more wary. She told herself he was probably just planning a surprise date night, something that they'd started off doing once a week early on in their marriage but had gradually slowed to random special occasions. Her eating disorder placed a strong strain on their relationship, and she appreciated that David put up with her problem, but as much as she liked spending time with no kids and just Dave, she also had grown to hate their alone time. The few-and-far-between dates they'd taken over the past five years started off with friendly chat and then turned into dark arguments about Sara's abnormal eating habits. The couple would go to bed angry and frustrated with one another, and it would take anywhere from twenty-four hours to five days for them to be able to have a calm, normal conversation again. The last few times these arguments had occurred, the make-up time had been closer to the five days rather than the twenty-four hours. It was hard to put on a loving face for the kids when this happened.

She rode along in silence as they dropped Cody and his two best friends off at the movie theater. One of the other moms was going to pick them up to spend the night, so she would have to face whatever David planned to say until Aimee arrived home at who knew what time. He hadn't given her a curfew. Sara felt a headache beginning to grow just thinking about her immediate future.

As soon as they pulled out of the theater's parking lot and onto the main road, David glanced over at her. "Would you like to grab dinner someplace?"

Sara quickly pondered the pretense she'd have to put on in a restaurant, of picking out something low-calorie to order, requesting extra napkins to hide the bites she spat out, rejecting a take-home box when the waitress looked at her full plate questioningly, and wasting money on food she wasn't actually swallowing—wasn't even really enjoying. The thought was exhausting and made her oncoming headache pound a little more fiercely. She smoothed out a wrinkle in her shirt and cleared her throat. "I'm not that hungry; you want to just pick up fast food or something for yourself, and we could go back home?"

The corners of David's mouth drooped as he watched the road, and Sara felt a twinge of sadness as she realized yet again that she'd disappointed him. She disappointed him so often anymore that she didn't feel as guilty as she used to, but she did still feel something. They'd been married for nearly twenty years, and she still loved him with all of her heart. That was why she worked hard to show her love in ways she could—by putting good meals on the table, taking care of their children, and keeping the house spotless. Her deep-seated fear of him leaving their marriage someday drew her to try to keep her anorexia hidden from Dave as much as possible, but she knew he was aware of more than he let on. She knew she couldn't live up to his expectations for her health, but she couldn't live up to her own expectations, either. Anymore, she didn't know what her goal weight should be. She knew going any lower than she already had might be too taxing on her health. She genuinely wanted to be around to celebrate their fiftieth wedding anniversary and to see her children grow up and have their own children. She didn't want to die young. The question from Ana's Servant burned on her conscience, and she knew she needed to answer it as soon as possible. She needed to be truthful about what could happen.

"I'll get Wendy's, I guess." He signaled to turn right, and Sara watched as a young family walked out of the restaurant, to-go bags in hand, smiling and laughing. She wished she could be that stress-free when it came to meal time.

As they pulled up to the drive-through, Dave asked one more time, "Are you sure you don't want anything?"

He was giving her the opportunity to redeem herself. Sara thought about her blog and about the fact that she had restarted the Rainbow Diet that day. She was supposed to be eating a cucumber for dinner. She tried to coax her tongue to say that she wanted something to eat, but all that came out was, "Yes, I'm sure."

The pain shot through Dave's eyes once again, and he turned to the intercom as the employee asked what he would like to order. He placed an order for his favorite sandwich and a medium fry, along with a large drink. He paused and glanced over at Sara again, then turned back to the intercom and tagged on a salad.

She pursed her lips.

He pulled forward, paid and collected the food, and they drove home in silence. As soon as Dave parked, Sara quickly unbuckled her seatbelt and darted ahead of him into the house. She wasn't sure where she was headed, but she did *not* want to be forced into eating that salad.

She ended up locking herself in the bathroom for ten minutes. Dave didn't say anything to her and didn't knock on the door. While she hung out in the bathroom, she weighed herself, touched up her makeup, turned sideways and lifted up her shirt to stare at her stomach for a moment three different times, and washed her feet off in the bathtub. They felt cold and clammy from being cooped up inside tennis shoes all day in the chilly soccer arena. She sat on the side of the tub, enjoying the warm water flowing over her slightly blue feet, and thought through what she could do to make the evening calm for both her and David. *I think I'll go slice up my cucumber and eat that with him in the living room. He can save the salad for Aimee if she's hungry when she gets home.* She toweled off and finally stepped out, avoiding the living room until she had a plateful of cucumber to take in with her. Dave sat in his usual chair, TV tray in front of him, sandwich nearly demolished and a puddle of ketchup spread out across the open wrapper. He dunked a fry and looked up at her as she walked into the room.

"I put your salad over there." He motioned to the chair where she normally sat. Another TV tray sat in front of that chair, salad popped open and dressing already carefully dispersed along the top. He had even opened up the plastic packet containing a disposable fork and knife and had set them on top of a napkin for her. A glass of water rested to the right of the food.

Sara sighed and sat down in her designated spot. She sipped at the water and slid the salad over to make room for the plate she'd brought in with her.

Dave finished his meal and the news over the course of the next five minutes and flicked off the TV. Sara nibbled at the cucumbers. In between bites she played with the salad, pushing the lettuce around with her fork and mixing the dressing onto every vegetable and piece of chicken in the entire bowl. She watched as he reached over to the coffee table beside him.

He picked up a colorful pamphlet and stared at it for a while. Sara couldn't read the words on it from where she sat.

She didn't have to wait long to find out what it was.

"Sara." Dave looked at her with the same pain in his eyes that had been there for years nearly every time he gazed her way. It spoke of love and sympathy and confusion and made her feel like a wounded baby animal. He crinkled the pamphlet in his hands, curling it into a cone and gently twisting.

I hate it when he's sad. Her love for him and a desire to make things right again overcame her plan to stick to only cucumbers for dinner. Sara prepped a bite of salad on her fork and stared at it for a couple of seconds before putting it in her mouth. She forced herself to chew. She chewed and chewed until it turned to slime in her mouth, but Dave kept looking at her, and she knew she wouldn't be able to subtly spit it into a napkin, so she loosened her jaw as best she could, took a few deep breaths in an effort to release the tightness in her throat, and forced herself to swallow. She couldn't help but mentally add up the calories as the ranch-dressing-laden missile crawled its way into her empty stomach.

"Sara, I love you so much, and I need you to listen to what I have to say. Please don't say anything until you hear me out, okay?"

She nodded tightly. Her fingers clenched around the plastic fork, and she stirred up the salad once more, careful not to spill any of its contents over the edge of the dish. She spied a piece of chicken that could be cut a little smaller, and she took her time slicing it in half. "What do you want to say, Dave?"

"I really, really want to find a way to help you, Sara. I know you're not happy. You keep getting thinner and thinner, and I'm concerned that if things continue to go the way they are, you're not going to be alive to celebrate our kids' graduations from high school. I know you don't want that." A tear slid from his eye. "I've been checking into local therapists and into rehab places for eating disorders, too. I know you think you've got this under control on your own, but I feel like I've given you long enough to get things figured out, and the situation only appears to be getting worse. Anymore I'm scared to hug you for fear I'm going to break you in half."

Sara kept her thoughts to herself but felt anger rising. How *dare* he try to tell her what to do. They were married, but it was *her* body, and she had every right to choose what she did or did not want to put in it. *Forget pretending to eat this salad.* She set her fork down.

"I've spent a lot of time doing research, and I've got it narrowed down to what seem to be the three best rehab locations and the three best therapists to handle eating disorders. I showed them to your mom, and she thought they seemed like great options, too."

He had shown them to her *mother*?! Sara could feel her face beginning to turn red. Still, she kept with her original agreement and did not respond to his invasion of her privacy.

"Sara, before you say anything, please think about how much it would hurt Aimee and Cody if you weren't around in two years. Or if you had some serious medical condition that stemmed from starving yourself, and you were alive but no longer able to be an active part of their lives. I know we don't get along the best all the time, and maybe you don't care anymore how it would affect me if you weren't around, but Sara, I love you. With all my heart. And I want to be able to enjoy as many years with you as I can. But right now I'm really scared—" his voice quivered, and another tear dropped out— "that I'm going to wake up one morning and you'll be dead from a heart attack in the bed beside me."

Her heart pounded erratically as if it really might be considering a heart attack, and her eyes welled up with tears. She absolutely hated when Dave cried about anything. She despised the idea that she was the cause of his sadness.

"Will you...please...for my sake and the kids' sake, if not for your own...get counseling of some sort for your eating disorder, whether through regular counseling or through actually going away for a while to a clinic?"

Sara tried to lighten the mood. "Am I allowed to talk now?" She smiled a little.

Dave smiled slightly in acquiescence.

"I...I don't really think I want counseling; I think I'm doing okay. And I *know* I don't want to go away to some rehab clinic. But...if it would make you feel better, I'll go to a counselor once a week, *for an hour*. I want to keep this from the kids, though. I don't want them to worry."

"Twice a week," Dave bargained.

"Dave." She glared at him.

"What if you go once, and we can ask the counselor if he or she thinks you need to visit more than once a week?"

Sara pondered the deal for a minute and finally nodded. "Okay. But do we agree that we won't tell the children? There's no real reason for them to find out. I can attend the appointments while they're in school."

"Yes, that makes sense for now. I think you need to tell them eventually, though."

"We'll see." Yeah, right. The kids, especially Cody, would interpret her as being psychotic. No, thanks. She didn't want her children to view her as though she was immature and needed looking after. No. She was the mom, and she took care of them. Not vice versa. She'd meet with this counselor a couple of times to satisfy Dave, and who knew. Maybe the counselor would actually help. She didn't know if she'd ever get to the point where she could eat three full meals a day like a "normal" person, but if she could eat even 1000 calories most days without feeling so guilty, it might be worth it. She looked down at her lap, her skinny jeans falling loosely to the sides around prominent bony thighs.

"Great. I'll call on Monday morning and set up your first appointment for you." Dave smiled, reached over, and squeezed her cold, pale hand. "Hon, you understand that I'm doing this because I love you, right? I think you're beautiful no matter what size you are, but I want you to be *healthy*."

She nodded and flipped her hand over to palm-side up so she could squeeze his hand back.

CHAPTER EIGHT

Aimee

When they arrived at Josh's friend's house, Aimee wasn't sure what to think. There were five cars parked in the driveway, and the house itself was large and a little nicer than Aimee's home (at least on the outside). Until now, Aimee had wondered if Josh's friends came from wealthy families or not. After all, wouldn't it be kind of weird to be a teenage millionaire and have friends who didn't even have enough of their own money to go get fast food with you? Friends who were dependent on a small allowance and most of whom didn't even have after-school jobs? If she had as much money as Josh did, she would be concerned that people only wanted to be friends with her because of her wealth.

As they walked up the driveway, Josh explained his friendship with Scott. "Scott and I have been best friends since first grade. When I lived around here, we used to have sleepovers all the time so that we could stay up all night to play video games. I only see him once every month or two now—

twice he's flown out to see me, and then usually my family comes back here to visit every two or three months, so that we can see my grandparents and other relatives."

They approached the front door and Josh rang the doorbell. So, he came back home every couple of months—if they kept in contact with each other, Aimee wouldn't get to see him that often. It could actually be the perfect relationship for her; she had a lot of things she liked to do on her own, and she usually spent a decent amount of time on homework each night to keep up her grades, so it could be good to be in a relationship with someone who lived further away and wouldn't be able to spend a lot of time with her. She smiled. It made her feel mature to be able to think of the distance as a good thing rather than being a clingy, love-struck teenager.

A messy-haired teen guy in a flannel threw open the front door and high-fived Josh. "Hey, man, good to see you! It's been a while."

"Hey, Scott," Josh replied. "How's it goin'?"

"Great, man. Everybody's downstairs if you want to come on down. Hi, I'm Scott," he said to Aimee, giving her a smile and a short wave.

Aimee started to introduce herself, but Josh stepped in. "This is Aimee. She interviewed me yesterday for her school newspaper and went to the concert with me when you backed out,"—he punched Scott in the shoulder—"so I thought she was a pretty good person to hang out with."

Aimee smiled, a little unsure about his description of her, and offered Scott her hand. He barely squeezed it when he shook it and motioned for them both to step inside the house. As she and Josh moved closer to Scott and he turned to lead them to the basement, she caught a huge whiff of cigarette smoke and wasn't certain if it was on Scott's clothes or if maybe the whole house smelled like that.

They made their way down the dark staircase, and Aimee was surprised that Josh, who was in front of her, half-turned and held out his hand to her. This was definitely a different situation than last night when he had grabbed her hand to guide her through the concert crowd. There was no real need to touch her at all at the moment. She wasn't getting lost in a group of people; she wasn't falling; and it wasn't even all that easy for him to hold her hand behind himself while he walked down the stairs. Aimee hesitated only briefly before accepting his offer. The feel of Josh's hand was warm and thrilling as they reached the bottom of the stairs, where he squeezed her hand and let go less than ten seconds after latching onto it. Her hand tingled as she drew it back to her side.

The staircase opened up into a shadowy basement, and Aimee had to wait a moment for her eyes to adjust to the darkness. The basement was like a separate apartment—there was a small kitchen on the end closest to the stairs, complete with a full-sized refrigerator and oven. The living room had two long couches and a multi-colored beanbag chair that looked nearly identical to one that Aimee had seen in her mom's college dorm pictures from the early '90s. The only light came from computer screens and a giant TV screen against the far wall. Two people sat in front of the TV, intensely building a house or something and yelling instructions at each other when their avatars were attacked. Were they all guys? Aimee took another quick scan of the dim room, searching for long hair or girly clothes or anything. She finally spotted a teen girl in the farthest, darkest corner who was chewing on a thumbnail as she stared intensely at a computer screen and hit the keys ferociously with her other hand. The girl looked to be within a couple of years of Aimee's age, was wearing big glasses with a punk-rocker haircut, and seemed more dedicated to the game than the guys were. Aimee's concerns about the day escalated. She was going to feel even more out of place than she had feared and was going to sit around bored. For hours.

She was debating calling her parents to see if one of them would come pick her up when Josh pulled a bag out from a kitchen cupboard. He set it on top of the counter and pulled out a laptop. "Have you ever played Minecraft, Aimee?"

She bit her lip and shook her head.

Scott laughed. "I'd say you're in for some intense training then."

Josh laughed as well and nodded in agreement.

Aimee smiled uncertainly, trying to be a good sport.

Josh powered up the laptop, dragged out a bar stool, and motioned for Aimee to take a seat. She accepted, feeling insecure and overwhelmed by the situation she had stepped into. Scott walked away to his own laptop and immediately became immersed in the same game all the others were playing, shouting and cursing when his avatar became injured.

Aimee looked over at the girl again. Maybe, if the girl ever looked up and took a break from her computer screen, Aimee could just go talk to her for a while. She wasn't certain she really wanted to learn this game.

There had been too much silence since either she or Josh had last spoken. It was getting awkward. Aimee cleared her throat. "You leave a computer here all the time?"

He chuckled. "Yeah, that way I don't have to bring it back and forth with me when I fly out here. Actually, a couple of the other computers in here are mine, too. They use them when I'm not here, and I don't really care, as long as they pay me back if they break them." He motioned to a guy sitting in the far corner. "That's Kaden—he has a bad temper and snapped one of my laptops in half last time I was here when we were playing Call of Duty. He just recently had enough money to pay me back, so now he can play again."

Aimee was surprised that Josh didn't seem angry by the fact that Kaden had destroyed one of his possessions. If she had a friend who broke her computer out of anger, Aimee would be furious and would question the friendship. But then again, Josh seemed to have a lot of computers—so many that he could just leave a few in a state he no longer lived in. "Hmm," she said. "That's really nice of you to share with them all like that."

Josh shrugged. "It's worth it; we have epic game sessions like this every time I come home. Before I bought the laptops, we'd have to all take turns sharing computers, and that got old." He settled onto the bar stool next to her and clicked his way through a few of the opening screens of the game. "Let's create your character. I'll show you how to play."

Over the next ten minutes, with Josh's help, Aimee created an avatar that looked nothing like her. The head was a giant cube, and all of the features were super pixellated. It was rather ugly.

As they neared the end of the avatar set-up, Scott suddenly called out, "Smoke break!"

Aimee's heart lurched in her chest. *Seriously?* Despite the cigarette scent that seemed to follow Scott around, Aimee hadn't realized that it was because he smoked. She had dismissed the smell, assuming that his parents smoked. Where were his parents, anyway? Surely they must have heard him announce that he was about to participate in an illegal activity. Aimee listened for footsteps from upstairs or an angry dad voice. Nothing. She glanced up from the computer screen as everybody responded to Scott's call, pausing their games and taking deep breaths, as though they had so much emotionally invested in the game that they had a difficult time being separated from it. Well, of course Josh wouldn't smoke, so she wouldn't be the only one refraining. *Are they going to laugh at me?* Her palms began sweating.

Scott pulled out a pack of cigarettes and took one, then passed the pack around the room. There were some kids at her high school who smoked, probably a lot actually, but Aimee didn't normally hang out with that crowd. She had never tried smoking and didn't want to do so. She wondered if any of the people in the room were of legal age to smoke. She knew Josh wasn't, and he had said that he and Scott had been best friends since elementary school, right? So Scott was likely the same age as Josh.

Everyone accepted a cigarette except the girl, and finally the pack made its way over to Josh and Aimee. Josh glanced at her briefly before pulling one out of the pack and then held the pack out to her. Aimee's mouth opened in surprise, but she stopped herself from scolding him. It wasn't her place to tell Josh what to do. She glanced over at the other girl again and shook her head. "I'm fine, but thank you."

He shrugged his shoulders, pulled a lighter out of his pocket as if he smoked all the time, and lit up. "Do you want to try it?"

Aimee shook her head again. This was a side of Josh she hadn't expected. *At least he's not doing drugs. Smoking is illegal, but only because he's not old enough yet.* She tried to relax. No one was laughing at her for choosing not to smoke. Maybe everything would be okay. The room was quiet for a moment as everyone drew in contaminated breaths. Aimee was startled at a rustle by her elbow. The girl had approached and was holding out a bag of Twizzlers. "Want one?"

Aimee smiled. "Sure, thanks." She pulled out a floppy red stick and stuck it in her mouth without thinking, grateful for something to do with her mouth and her hands while everyone else enjoyed their carcinogens. The girl settled on the bar stool next to her and set the bag on the countertop, biting off the tops of two Twizzlers.

As soon as the sweet, cherry-flavored candy hit her tongue, Aimee's head was filled with thoughts of calories and ingredients. This wasn't healthy; it was full of red food dye and sugar. And junk food always contained a lot of calories. She stared at the bag on the counter. Well, it did say low fat. She sucked on the candy as she pondered what to do and subtly scanned for a trash can. The girl had pulled out another piece and was halfway through it. As if voicing its opinion, Aimee's stomach growled loudly, requesting that she swallow the candy and give it something to digest. The girl laughed and pushed the bag closer to Aimee as Aimee felt her face turn red.

"Have as many pieces as you want," the girl said. "You could use some extra weight. I'm Kara. What's your name?" She shoved her glasses up further on her nose.

Aimee pulled the candy out of her mouth to answer. "Aimee. Thank you," she mumbled. She quickly stuck the licorice back in her mouth when she realized it probably looked weird that she hadn't taken even one bite, especially when her stomach had betrayed her by announcing its emptiness. There was no trash can nearby and no napkin to hide the candy. She gave in and nibbled on it.

It was as if a floodgate had opened. By the time the "smoke break" was over, together Aimee and Kara had consumed half of the large bag of licorice. Aimee blinked at the bag, worriedly trying to add up how many pieces of candy she had just mindlessly shoved into her mouth. *Wait, what am I doing? I'm allowed to eat whatever I want—the experiment is over,* she reminded herself.

Right, but weren't you trying to eat healthier so you can stay thin?

Yes, she conceded. And she had just given in to her hunger and consumed who knew how many pieces of sugary candy—ten, twelve? Maybe more. The thought made her sway on her bar stool.

Josh reached over and took a Twizzler from the bag. "Wow, ladies, are you going to share any with the rest of us?"

Aimee's heart plummeted, and she wondered if Josh thought she was a pig.

Kara stuck out her tongue at him. "You were too busy with your cigarette."

He ground out the butt of the cigarette in a glass ashtray. "Yeah, I guess so."

After a couple more minutes, the gaming resumed. By the end of the night, Aimee had become fairly skilled at Minecraft and was having fun. The rest of the group took a few more smoke breaks, but she managed to stay away from both the tobacco and the candy, even after a bag of miniature candy bars appeared. They ordered pizza at one point, but Aimee only took the tiniest slice of cheese pizza and sipped water. So much water. She had been visiting the bathroom nearly every hour while at Scott's house because she was using water as a way to avoid the consumption of more junk food. She hated that she felt guilty while eating the pizza, even though she stopped eating once she reached the part that was just crust. Josh tried to get her to eat more, but it wasn't too hard to beg out of it, considering that the room was full of "starving" teenage guys. All six large pizzas were gone in less than twenty minutes. Josh teased her again about filling up on the

Twizzlers, and even though she knew he was just kidding and in no way meant to hurt her feelings, she still felt a little twinge of shame at having stuffed her face with junk food. The candy was certainly not going to help her achieve her goal of being healthy. It made her feel bloated just thinking about it.

It was nearly midnight when Aimee pulled her phone out of her purse and was shocked to see that her parents had not tried to contact her. *What is going on with them lately?* First, they'd let her go to a concert with Josh and stay out late, and now, the very next night, they let her hang out with him again and hadn't given her any sort of a curfew. They still hadn't even met him. Although she enjoyed the freedom and the trust that it implied, Aimee was also concerned that there might be a problem she didn't know about. Her mom seemed to be getting a lot of headaches lately—could there be a serious, underlying health issue that her parents were keeping secret from Aimee and Cody? She should go home and check on her mom. A couple of people had left already, and so maybe Josh would be okay with leaving, too. Or, if he could just take Aimee home, he could even come back to Scott's house and play video games all night—it was his life; he could do whatever he wanted. She glanced over at him, about to say something, when all of a sudden he straightened up and stretched. "Well, should we head on out, Aimee? It's getting kind of late—I don't want your parents to get angry."

She nodded and lifted her purse off the countertop. "Yeah, I'm getting tired, anyway."

"Me, too." He closed the laptop and put it back in its bag. "Thanks for the party, Scott."

Scott paused in his game to stand up and bump fists with Josh and then turned to Aimee to do the same. She wasn't expecting this gesture and stared at him blankly for a split second before hurriedly raising her hand to meet his, laughing nervously. "Nice to meet you, Scott."

"You too, Aimee." He smiled and returned to playing.

Josh led the way up the stairs and out the front door. As Aimee stepped onto the porch, he turned to her and held out his hand. She took it cautiously, feeling her cheeks turn red. He smiled and pulled her alongside him to walk back to the car. The full moon lit up the yard and reflected off the dewy windshields of the vehicles in the driveway.

"Thanks for coming with me," Josh said quietly, clicking open the locks with his car remote.

"Yeah, it was fun," Aimee said. "Honestly, I wasn't sure about playing video games, but you were a good teacher. I feel like I somewhat know what I'm doing now." She turned and smiled at him. They had arrived at the car, and Josh's free hand rested on the handle of the passenger door.

"Good." He glanced away, looking anxious, and Aimee stared at his hand, willing him to either open the door for her or let her open it herself. She was freezing.

She shifted her gaze back to his eyes and found him staring at her. Her breath caught in her throat as he began to lean a little closer. *Oh my goodness, he's going to kiss me! Do I want him to kiss me? I don't even know how to kiss!* Was she going to completely embarrass herself in front of this wealthy genius? Was anybody watching from the house? She wanted to see if anyone was looking through the front windows but was scared she would miss his mouth if she lost concentration for even a split second. Her stomach squirmed, and she wondered if maybe it wasn't a good idea to have her first kiss with a guy she'd known for barely more than 24 hours. She had always pictured herself dating someone for, well…at least a few weeks (months, maybe?) before kissing. *A first kiss should be special.*

He kept coming in closer, and she stood right where she was, wondering if she should lean in, too. What if he wasn't intending to kiss her, and she leaned in? That would be even more embarrassing than being a poor kisser. Suddenly his lips were right in front of her mouth, and the fear of kissing him incorrectly won out. Aimee turned her head so that his kiss landed on her cheek. It was quick, and she was vaguely aware that his breath reeked of tobacco. She sensed Josh's hesitation in the moment after, and he cleared his throat. Aimee didn't meet his eyes but stared down at his hand on the car.

He finally opened her door, and she slid inside.

CHAPTER NINE

Aimee

As Josh started the car and pulled out of Scott's driveway, Aimee wondered what to say. She wondered if Josh was angry with her for ducking his kiss and if maybe this would be the last time they would hang out. As soon as they were on the road, he turned on the radio, and they drove in silence for a couple of minutes.

"You did well at Minecraft." Josh's quiet voice could barely be heard over the music.

"Thanks." Aimee propped her elbow on the car door and stared out at the street signs rolling past. "I had a good time." She hoped the statement would bridge the gap between them and let him know that just because she'd dodged the kiss tonight didn't mean that she wished to stop being his friend. Josh's smoking had definitely been a surprise, and she didn't approve of it; but something in her still liked him and craved his attention.

He didn't respond, and Aimee figured things were over

between them. Regret poured into her heart and dried into heavy cement. She swallowed back tears. *I shouldn't be upset—we barely know each other. But even though he might not be the best choice, he is the closest thing I've ever had to a boyfriend, and I really like him.*

The house was dark and quiet when Aimee arrived home. Josh told her goodbye and did not attempt another kiss. Her parents had left a single living room lamp on to help guide her way, but no one was awake. She had really been hoping her mom would be awake, like last night, so that she could ask her if everything was all right. She was growing more and more concerned that the freedom her normally strict parents had been allowing her was not so much an indication that they trusted her (though they should—after all, she hadn't given in and smoked) but rather a clue that something was wrong. Could they be getting a divorce? They hadn't talked to each other much lately, and they almost never participated in family events together anymore, other than sitting with each other at Cody's soccer games. Usually Aimee and Cody hung out with one parent or the other, as opposed to the whole family experiencing life together the way they used to when Aimee and Cody were small. The older Aimee grew, the more she had become scared that her parents would split up the way many of her friends' parents had. She rarely heard them argue, but the lack of communication between them indicated that there could be serious problems lurking under the surface.

She didn't understand why. Her mom seemed to do everything, plus more, that a stereotypical "good" housewife should. Her dad worked hard but didn't work overly long hours, so he was usually available whenever they needed him for something and always showed up to their school programs, games, and recitals. The family didn't seem to have any money problems—Aimee knew they certainly didn't have as much money as Josh did, but there always seemed to be enough for little extras, and they lived in an average-sized house. They even took a vacation once a year. Her dad bought her mom flowers a few times a year, more often than just for their anniversary and Valentine's Day. To others, it probably seemed as though Aimee had a nearly perfect family. But she just couldn't let go of the feeling that something was wrong. She needed to figure out the best way to approach the topic and get some answers.

*****

Sunday was church day. Aimee had an especially tough time rolling out of bed after two late nights in a row. Cody ended up opening her bedroom door and sending the dog in to jump on top of her to "help" her wake up. Aimee sat up, furious, as Treasure licked her face and stepped his heavy self all over her empty stomach. "Cody!"

She could hear him snickering as he walked down the hall.

"Treasure, I love you, buddy, but you need to settle down." She gently but forcefully pushed the dog into a sitting position beside her on the bed. His tail continued to wag as he panted from the exertion of treating her like a piece of earth. She stroked his fur a couple of times as she yawned and looked over at her alarm clock. She only had twenty-five minutes to get ready before they would leave for church. Aimee forced herself to throw the covers aside and gather up her robe and makeup bag for the bathroom. As she hurried to the shower, black spots danced before her eyes, but she sucked in a deep breath and kept going. *I should probably eat something before church.*

She sped through washing her hair, despite the dull headache creeping around the back of her skull. *Uggghhh, I hope*

ANGELA BACON GRIMM

I can get a nap today. Dizziness joined the headache while she combed out her hair and applied her makeup. She had to stop occasionally to grip the bathroom counter. *I'm fine, just hungry,* she told herself.

Aimee made it downstairs with dripping hair just as everybody else was putting on their coats. She ducked into the kitchen to see if there was anything healthy she could grab to eat in the car. An orange caught her attention, but she didn't want to have sticky fingers once she reached church and had to shake hands with everybody. She popped open cupboard doors and spied a box of Special K bars. Only 90 calories each. Special K products were supposed to be healthy, right? She snatched one and threw her arms into her coat as her dad started up the car in the garage.

Cody was frantically studying his Bible verses for Sunday school. Aimee had never seen him do anything so intently. "That's great you're learning your verses, Cody, but why the sudden interest?"

"Mrs. Griswold said she would have a surprise for everyone who could recite these three verses this week." He pointed to the verses in a frustrated motion without removing his eyes from them. "Shhhh."

Aimee laughed. "It's probably just candy or something little, Cody. Remember what you used to get in Awana?"

He glared at her. "Be quiet. I don't know what the surprise is, so I want to learn my verses just in case it's something important."

Aimee stifled a laugh and ripped open her Special K bar.

"Cody, you should have worked on them sooner," their mom said gently from the front seat. "I offered to practice them with you on Thursday, remember?"

"Hmmmmmph," Cody mumbled, running his finger

104

across the page and then staring up at the ceiling of the car as he mouthed the words silently.

Aimee bit into the top of the frosting-drizzled bar and studied the ingredients on the back of the wrapper while she chewed. Although the bar only contained 90 measly calories, the list of ingredients was surprisingly long and included a lot of sugar. What a farce. Not healthy at all. She frowned at the bar and debated whether to put any more of it into her body.

Her dad looked at Aimee and Cody in the rearview mirror. "You guys are extra quiet this morning."

She saw Cody screw up his face and bite his lip to keep from commenting angrily on how everybody was disturbing his review time. She decided to be a nice big sister and bail him out.

"I'm just tired."

"Did you have fun last night?"

"Yes, I did, actually. I learned how to play Minecraft. I didn't think I'd like it, but it turned out to be kind of fun." She left out the smoking and the part about Josh trying to kiss her. It wasn't like she'd done anything wrong. Although…she kind of wondered if she would have tried a cigarette if there had been any real pressure to do so. Kara had graciously given her an out with the Twizzlers, and Josh didn't appear to be the type to hardcore pressure anyone into anything. In the light of day, she was able to think more rationally about the situation and was mostly glad she had rejected his kiss. If he wanted to stop seeing her because of that rejection, then she would just have to find a way to be okay with it. They had only known each other for a couple of days, and she simply didn't want to give her first kiss away to a stranger. She did feel a little left out, though, because at least half of the girls in her class claimed to have experienced their first kiss way back in middle school.

"I can't believe you actually figured out how to play," Cody muttered in between reciting verses.

Aimee resisted sticking out her tongue at him and looked down at her cereal bar. She shuddered at the thought of the ingredients again, took one more tiny bite, and then wrapped it back up and set it on the floor. Fine. This reset of healthy eating was difficult. There didn't seem to be much available that was healthy enough. She would just deal with an empty stomach and wait until after church to fill up.

Once in the church building, Sara beelined to the coffeemaker, and Aimee followed. She didn't normally drink coffee, but besides feeling tired today, she really wanted to put something in her stomach. *Coffee only has two calories*, she reminded herself, then wondered why that information should even matter anymore now that her experiment was over.

As Sara poured herself a cup, she looked over and noticed her daughter beside her. "Aimee. You really shouldn't start this habit."

"I'm not starting a habit, I just want a cup today," Aimee argued. "It's not a big deal."

Sara sighed. "You see how addicted I am to it. I end up with a migraine if I skip coffee for one morning."

"Yes, Mom, I know. Like I said, I just want one cup today." Aimee took the handle of the pot that her mother had just set down and poured herself a full Styrofoam cup, dousing the steaming liquid with cream and sugar. This reaction from her mom was the kind she was used to. The freedom her parents had allowed her the past two days was unusual. *What is going on with them?*

"I don't want you to start drinking it every day at home." Sara sipped on her own coffee, tension visibly disappearing as she breathed in the fumes.

"I know." Irritated, Aimee took a sip and a quick peek around the room to see if anyone was standing close enough to hear the way her mom was embarrassing her. She had put so much cream in it that it actually tasted all right. *Wait. Cream.* That probably wasn't healthy, was it? And the sugar, so much sugar. She hadn't even thought about it while dumping the two extras in, but her black coffee with two calories had gone from an acceptable beverage to junk food rather quickly. Uggghhh, would she never learn? Now what would she do? Her throat seemed to close up at the thought of consuming more junk, especially after the Twizzlers she had binge-eaten the night before. *It is soooo hard to eat healthy.* Aimee felt tears coming on, which surprised her. She normally controlled her emotions well. But for some reason, staring at that tainted coffee, she felt a real fear. A little bit of it was a fear of gaining weight, and the larger part of it was a fear of being unhealthy. This wasn't an eating disorder; it was merely a realization that most of what she ate on a regular basis was not helpful to her body. She felt her khakis slide down a bit on her hips. Even though she had only been dieting for a few days, she was definitely noticing a difference in the fit of her clothing. Aimee knew she wasn't dangerously thin, not by any means. In fact, before she'd begun her newspaper experiment, she had been nearly ten pounds overweight for her height. All she wanted to do was get a flatter stomach and maybe get down to normal weight for her height, all while being conscious of whether what she was eating was a healthy choice or not. There was nothing wrong with that desire.

Her mother had always been thin. *I want to be thin like Mom.* The steam from the warm cup cradled in Aimee's hands heated her face as she watched Sara grab a church bulletin from the table.

In Sunday school, she had a hard time concentrating. Aimee never really liked Sunday school. Her high school Sunday school class only had between seven and ten students in attendance on average, and most of them were incredibly nerdy, immature guys. When it came down to it, Aimee liked hanging out with nerds (as evidenced by Josh), but she couldn't stand immaturity. The couple of girls who attended class spent much of the Sunday school hour quietly gossiping and passing notes back and forth. Aimee usually said hi to them and then left them alone the rest of the time.

On the way to the auditorium for the church service, Aimee began to feel dizzy again. She walked close to the wall so that she could lean against it if need be to steady herself. The coolness of the bricks occasionally brushing her arm was soothing. She stopped at the drinking fountain and sucked down several gulps of water before sitting with her parents and Cody. While they were all standing for the first song, the dizziness drastically increased, and she sat down on the pew without fully realizing what she was doing. Her head spun as she leaned forward and gripped her scalp, willing her body to behave.

Sara bent down next to her and put a hand on her back. "Aimee, are you okay? Are you sick?"

She squeezed her eyes shut and rubbed her forehead, and things had started to clear up a little when she dared to look at the world again. "I think I'm okay. I got kind of lightheaded." Aimee turned to look into her mom's worried eyes. "I might just sit a couple more minutes."

"Do you feel like you're going to throw up?" her mom asked.

Aimee felt her cheeks burn, even though she knew

probably no one else could hear Sara over all of the singing voices and musical instruments.

"I'm fine," Aimee insisted. "Just…hungry or something, probably. I should have gotten up sooner so I could have eaten breakfast."

"Did you eat dinner last night with Josh?"

"Yes, well, kind of."

"Okay. I'll sit with you until you feel better."

Truth be told, her mom didn't look all that well herself. Her face was pale, and even though she wore a decent amount of makeup, Aimee could still clearly see dark circles under her eyes. She grew concerned about the situation between her parents all over again and whether or not they might be hiding something from her and Cody. Concentrating on that topic made her regain focus, and she slowly straightened up as the dizziness faded away. By this time, the singing was over and everyone else was taking a seat anyway, so she didn't have to try to stand again.

The sermon was about treating your body like God's temple, and this message convinced Aimee even more that she was doing the right thing by trying to stay away from unhealthy food. God would want her to take the best care of her body that she could, and she could do that by exercising and severely restricting what junk food entered her body so that she could get down to a healthy weight.

CHAPTER TEN

Sara

Sara dreaded dropping the kids off at school on Monday. It meant that as soon as she was alone, she had to fulfill her promise to Dave to attend her first counseling session in years. She didn't want to talk to anybody about her eating disorder—to admit that she had lost control over her eating habits half a lifetime ago. Saturday night, though, Dave had told her that either she could attend counseling sessions once a week in secret from their children or they could tell the children together about her eating disorder, and she could go away to rehab for a while. No way was she picking the second option. Risk losing the respect of her children and have them thinking she was some kind of mental case? No, thank you. Besides, she wasn't nearly as bad as some of the anorexics out there. She wasn't even close to being deathly thin or anything dangerous like that.

Sara wanted to be fixed—she really did. She hated that so much of her life and her thoughts centered on eating and staying thin. But she had also grown to love the attention her blog received. It made her feel important, even if that feeling came from something unhealthy. If the therapist truly ended up helping her with her eating disorder (and she knew she needed to make a valiant effort, otherwise Dave was going to tell the kids about her anorexia and send her away), she would have to give up her blog audience. Maybe she could start blogging about something else...she racked her brain, but sadly, the only thing she felt as though she was an expert at was living life as an anorexic. No one was going to want to hear about her life as a normal, stay-at-home mom. The only thing "unique" that she seemed to have going for her was her eating disorder, and that was a downright depressing realization.

Sara ducked into the downstairs bathroom to touch up her hair before she had to leave for her appointment with the psychologist. She carefully re-arranged the section above her right ear to hide her bald spot, the bare section that had developed in the last few years as her hair had begun falling out. It was a common symptom of anorexia, Sara knew, and she wasn't that worried about it. As long as she used plenty of hair spray, her hair stayed in place and covered up the empty section. The pieces that came out in her fingers as she washed her hair every morning blended into the drain with Aimee's long hair.

Lengthy hair-spraying session complete, she used a Q-tip to touch up her eyeliner and walked out to the car. She had forced herself to eat that morning, as she figured the psychologist would probably ask about her breakfast. It wasn't much, but it was far more than she normally ate—Sara had coaxed her throat to swallow half of a piece of toast with a thin spread of peanut butter on it. *Rainbow Diet plan foiled again.* The peanut butter had nearly gagged her, but she had purposely eaten at the table with her kids because she was always able to make herself do more if Cody and Aimee were present and watching. She didn't want to cause any doubts in their minds about her good health. Even so, she couldn't help but feel nauseous at the thought of so many calories swimming around in her stomach, all before 8 a.m. Unless this psychologist was really good, she probably wouldn't eat the rest of the day.

She pulled into the parking lot of the doctor's office and forced herself to take deep breaths to calm down. Part of her wished she had made Dave promise to attend these sessions with her. The other part of her didn't want him to be aware of just how little she was eating.

The psychologist looked young, and Sara's doubts came back in full force. How could this woman possibly be able to help her? She looked fresh out of college. The woman smiled and shook her hand. Her red hair glinted in the light. "I'm Dr. Renner," she said with a Chicago accent. "Please take a seat."

"I'm Sara," Sara replied and obeyed.

Dr. Renner sat down as well and straightened her suit jacket before taking a manila folder and a pen from her desk. "So, Sara, I thought today we would just get to know each other a bit. Tell me about your family."

That was easy. Sara spoke about her children and their accomplishments at school and extracurricular activities, and she also spoke lovingly of her husband's great work ethic. Dr. Renner, in turn, told Sara about her own life for a few moments and even showed Sara a picture of her three-year-old daughter. The only part of the session in which Dr. Renner touched on Sara's eating disorder was when she asked her what the circumstances were surrounding the beginning of Sara's extreme dieting.

Sara felt her throat constrict as if she was going to have to eat peanut butter again. They had been talking for nearly half an hour, and Sara had been able to relax and almost forget the reason she was meeting with this woman in the first place. She cleared her throat, trying to sound like the question had not affected her. "I was thirteen. My mom was always drinking SlimFast and eating salads for every meal. Although I wouldn't call her anorexic, I never saw her weigh more than what I would say is average for her height. She always dressed nicely, and she always looked perfect. When I started puberty and began to feel chubby, she never told me I was fat but did begin to substitute salads for my school lunches and many of my dinners. One of my friends, Rachel, who was heavier than I was, started talking about the things she was doing to lose weight. Once I noticed that her clothes were getting baggier and her diet really seemed to be paying off, I asked her about her weight loss tips in more detail. Basically, she chewed gum a lot, smoked sometimes, and only ate when people were watching, like lunch at school and suppertime at home. Rachel's parents both left for work every morning before she had to go to school, so nobody was ever around to watch if she ate breakfast or not. She never allowed herself to have snacks or dessert. I didn't want to smoke to stay thin—I knew my mom would kill me if she smelled smoke on my clothes— but I did adopt my friend's other dieting habits. I began spending my babysitting money on SlimFast and kept a big canister of it in my locker to mix with water—that was how you bought it in the '80s. Many times I would throw my bagged lunch away at school and drink SlimFast instead. After all, my mom drank it, and she seemed to stay thin and healthy, so I figured I may as well drink it, too. I always ate dinner because my whole family ate supper together religiously every night, and someone would have noticed if I quit eating. Overall, my plan was working. I was hungry a lot of the time, but because I was still eating, I didn't feel too many ill effects of dieting. I lost seven pounds, but then I couldn't seem to lose any more weight. Rachel kept losing pounds and soon was down to my size.

"At this point, her parents were in the middle of a divorce, and no one was keeping track of whether or not she ate at all. I was so jealous of her when she would come to homeroom in the morning and tell me she hadn't eaten dinner the night before. She would tell me about the new clothes she'd bought, each time a size smaller than the shopping trip before, and soon I renewed my commitment to dieting. I began drinking only half a serving of SlimFast at lunch and at dinner I started taking smaller portions, focusing mostly on whatever vegetable my mom had cooked that night. For breakfast, to satisfy my mom's insistence that we kids put something in our stomachs so we could concentrate at school, I always ate either a banana or an apple. I would say at this point I was consuming probably around 800 calories a day, maybe less."

Dr. Renner nodded, and Sara continued.

"Rachel kept getting more and more strict with her dieting, and many times she would go four or five days in a row without food, just water. She ended up in the hospital for malnutrition. Even though I could see how her anorexia was hurting her, I was hooked at this point. I couldn't stop restricting my calories. It was like a game every day, to see if I had the willpower to eat less than the day before. Rachel gained a little weight after staying in the hospital and then subsequently meeting with a psychologist for a few weeks, but once her parents let her quit going to the appointments, she went right back to dieting with me. One morning, her mom couldn't wake her up for school. She had suffered a heart attack in the night caused by her anorexia and died, all alone, without anyone realizing what was going on."

CHAPTER ELEVEN

Aimee

Mrs. Bennett gave Aimee high praise for her article in class on Monday. "You really asked Josh some great questions, Aimee! I think a lot of people are going to find this article fascinating. This will look great on the front page."

Aimee, despite feeling worn out and hungry, beamed at her teacher's compliments and could feel Kirsten's glare across the room. So what? Kirsten had given up her assignment—she could have been the one to be "teacher's pet" but punked out to go on a date. Aimee was definitely feeling the benefits of being responsible—besides writing a front-page article, she had been able to go on *two* dates. With a millionaire. Granted, she hadn't heard from Josh since he had dropped her off at home Saturday night (which bothered her more than she cared to admit), but overall, it had been a great weekend. Aimee was tempted to text him but was trying to resist the urge. Should she have let him kiss her on Saturday? Part of her regretted dodging the kiss now that Josh had been silent for a while, but she kept trying to convince herself that she shouldn't kiss someone out of pressure or fear of what that person would think of her. She struggled to remember what day Josh had said he was heading back home—today? Tomorrow? Aimee held out a bit of hope that she would get to see him again before he left the state. The fact that he smoked still niggled at her conscience a little, but again, he probably wasn't addicted to it. She hadn't seen him smoke at all on Friday, and he hadn't smoked on Saturday until they were at Scott's house. It was probably just a thing he did with friends. And cigarettes, although bad for one's health, weren't anything illegal once you were eighteen. It wasn't like she'd witnessed him snorting cocaine or anything.

Kirsten stopped her as everybody was gathering up their stuff to leave class. "So I take it the interview went well? Was Josh nice?"

"Yeah, I had a lot of fun at the interview. Josh was super nice." Aimee debated how much to tell Kirsten. "I ended up going to a concert with him after the interview because his friend backed out last-minute." She left off the part about seeing him on Saturday. Gaming with his nerdy friends didn't sound as cool and impressive as going to a concert for free with him.

Kirsten raised her eyebrows. "No way! That's awesome. I should have done the interview—my date with Trey sucked. We went to Burger King, where he realized he'd forgotten his wallet, and I paid for everything. We were supposed to go to a movie after, but then there wasn't enough time to go back home and pick up his wallet before the movie started, and I didn't have enough money on me to pay for the food *and* the tickets. I haven't heard from him since Friday, and I have a feeling he's never going to pay me back. What a waste." She pouted her glossy lips.

"Oh, that's too bad," Aimee cooed sympathetically, secretly thrilled that her weekend had been so much better than Kirsten's.

"Well, thanks again for helping me out," Kirsten said and walked away.

Aimee made it through the day, eating a salad with no dressing at lunch (but still a plateful of food, nonetheless) and carefully avoiding all of the processed toppings at the salad bar. She ended up with just a huge plateful of lettuce and spinach, some sunflower seeds, carrots, and cucumbers. The available ham and turkey to put on top were just chunks of heavily processed lunch meat, and the black bucket of cheese was empty by the time she made it through the line. She figured the bacon bits weren't real bacon, and things like croutons and crunchy chow mein noodles couldn't possibly improve her health. Unfortunately, the dry salad with little flavor was not especially appealing to her tastebuds.

Meghan and Coralee seemed low on gossip today, so Aimee shared her experiences with Josh over the weekend and asked if they thought she should text him. She had secretly typed out a short text to him while standing in the lunch line but hadn't sent it yet.

"I would," Coralee said. "It can't hurt just to text him once. He sounds great! I want to meet him."

Meghan looked thoughtful while she chewed her sandwich. "Yeah, I say go for it."

Aimee pulled her phone out of her pocket and studied her text one more time before sending it off.

Hey, hope your day is going well!

She spent the rest of the lunch period dutifully chewing and swallowing her meal, but by the time lunch was dismissed, a third of her plate was still present. It wasn't really her intention to stay under a certain number of calories, but by eliminating everything that looked as though it could potentially be unhealthy, she had ruled out a lot of foods with high calorie content. She checked her phone at least a dozen times before the bell rang, but Josh never texted her back. Worry began to chip away at her rational thoughts. Had she completely ruined the possibility of seeing Josh again?

She was hungry an hour after lunch but had no opportunity to eat until she arrived home at 3:30. She scanned the cupboards and fridge while her mom quietly prepared dinner. "Is it all right if I eat these?" she asked, holding up a plastic carton of strawberries.

Sara jumped a little, as if she hadn't even realized that someone else was in the kitchen with her until now. "Sure, that's fine, Aimee."

"What's for dinner?" Aimee scrutinized the items on the counter, carefully evaluating the health value of each product.

"Fried chicken, baked potatoes, and salad." Sara scrubbed a potato underneath the running water as she spoke.

"Hmmm, okay." Aimee loved fried chicken but knew that something fried was not health-conscious at all. Maybe she could pick the crispy skin off. She would eat a baked potato, too. And some salad. Again.

She anxiously waited for her mom to finish cleaning the potatoes so she could wash her strawberries off. Task completed a few minutes later, Aimee went upstairs and felt a rush of adrenaline upon finding a text from Josh. Was it possible that he was interested in her despite Saturday's incident?

Aimee, are you up for hanging out tonight?

She popped a berry in her mouth and evaluated what to reply. She wanted to sound eager but not obsessed with him.

Yes, of course! I have to do a little bit of homework, but then I should be able to see you tonight.

Aimee smiled as she typed and grinned even more when he took just a couple of seconds to respond.

Great! I'll pick you up at 6. Make sure you're hungry ☺

She had just finished up an entire container of strawberries but was still plenty hungry. Still, she wondered where he was taking her and whether she'd be able to order something healthy. Her palms grew clammy just thinking about it. Aimee didn't want to cause a scene in a restaurant by asking about ingredients in certain dishes, or cause Josh to think she was crazy because she wanted plain food. Should she ask where they were going, or let it be a surprise and just go with the flow once they arrived at the restaurant? She didn't want Josh to think she was annoying if she asked too many questions, so she refrained and simply said okay.

Aimee quickly finished up her history reading for the next day. She had some time left to do more research for her anorexia article, but after checking for updated entries on some of the blogs she'd found the previous week, Aimee found her interest pulled toward sites about healthy eating. It was discouraging how far away from nutritious her normal eating habits were. At five o' clock she went downstairs to tell her family she wouldn't be eating dinner with them.

Sara smiled at her when she walked into the kitchen. "Aimee, I was just about to call you down here." She set a plate of baked potatoes on the dining room table.

"Thanks, Mom, but I'm going out to eat with Josh again." Aimee set the bowl from her strawberries into the kitchen sink with the other dirty dishes.

"Oh, really?" Her mom gave her a mischievous grin. "We'd like to meet Josh, you know."

"I think he flies back to New York tomorrow. He just wants to hang out one last time before he goes back. I'm not sure how long it'll be before he's in Michigan again." Aimee shrugged, wanting to tell her mom it was no big deal, but at the same time thinking about Saturday's almost kiss. She blushed and stared down at her hands, fidgeting on the top of the chair she leaned against. "When he gets here tonight, I'll see if he has time to come in and say hi. I'm not sure what his plans are for tonight, whether he has reservations or anything, so there might not be extra time."

She had mixed feelings about Josh meeting her parents. Her parents had always met her friends, and her friends had always seemed to like her parents. But if Josh came in to talk to them, that implied there was something serious going on, and they had only known each other for a few days. She felt like Josh was giving her a second chance after Saturday's awkwardness, and she wondered if he would attempt to kiss her again that evening.

She went back upstairs to change clothes and touch up her hair and makeup. She found a fitted shirt she hadn't worn in a couple of months, and when she put it on, she rejoiced at how thin it made her look. She turned again and again in front of the mirror, putting her hands on her hips and pretending to be a model. She dug out some leggings, which she knew would smooth out her stomach even more, and found her black boots that came up nearly to her knee. This was the most effort she had put into an outfit since meeting Josh, and she hoped he liked it. She darkened her eye makeup a bit but not too much because she figured it might make her dad freak out. Aimee was brushing her hair again when she heard the doorbell ring.

She flew down the stairs to try to get to the door before anyone else in her family did, but her dad was already greeting Josh. *So much for being indecisive about Mom and Dad meeting him.* Her mom walked up behind her as Aimee tried to get between her dad and Josh, and she could hear Cody yakking in the background about wanting to meet him, too. *Great.*

Josh looked pleased to see her and not overwhelmed by her family's presence. He ended up stepping into the entryway and talking with her family for ten minutes. Cody even praised him for how great Tyrannosaurus Scoop was.

"So where are you guys going tonight?" her dad eventually asked. He crossed his arms and looked from Josh to Aimee and back again. The jovial mood of moments earlier had passed, and Dave was back to being what Aimee had expected—the suspicious, overprotective parent.

"Out to eat," Josh said smoothly. "Don't worry, I won't keep her out late. I know it's a school night."

Aimee stuck out her tongue at him. He made her sound like such an infant.

"Aimee, we do want you to be home by ten," her dad said.

"That's fine. I will be." Aimee stepped forward to stand

next to Josh. "I'll see you guys later."

"Nice to meet you all," Josh said before following Aimee out the door.

Once in the car, Aimee sighed. "Sorry about that. They were giving me a hard time tonight about the fact that they hadn't met you."

"Oh, that's okay. Your family seems really nice," Josh said as he pulled away from the curb. "So, we're going to check out a place I've never been before. The food is supposed to be really good."

"Okay." Aimee watched the houses and trees roll by and speed on past as they pulled onto the expressway. "What's the name of it?" *I guess he's over what happened on Saturday. Good.*

"Lochlomond's."

"Where is that? I've never even heard of it."

"It's in the Tiger Trail Casino." He said it nonchalantly and glanced over at her as he switched lanes. "In Battle Creek."

"The casino?" Aimee's heart fluttered. "But we aren't old enough to go to a casino."

"At this particular one you only have to be eighteen, not twenty-one."

"Ummmm, neither one of us is eighteen. You're seventeen, right?"

"Don't worry, I took care of it."

Aimee wanted to ask more questions but also didn't want to sound immature. Maybe "I took care of it" meant that the casino was okay with them just eating, as long as they didn't gamble? He must have already talked to the manager or something. It would be okay. Josh had a lot of money—he probably had connections somehow.

It took another thirty minutes to drive to the casino, and Aimee was shocked at how packed the parking lot was. Once

Josh had finally found a parking spot, he reached into his wallet and pulled out a Michigan ID and handed it to Aimee. She gasped when she saw her own face on the ID, with a birthdate of three years older than she actually was.

Josh grinned. "Do you like it?"

She bit her lip. "What? How did you…?"

"I found this picture of you on Instagram. Scott knows someone who makes fakes, so I talked to him and paid for both of us to have fakes made. See?" He held up another ID with his own face on it, his birthdate claiming he was nineteen.

"Josh, I…I…" She had no desire to use this ID. To test it and see if security allowed her to enter the casino or not. But Josh had gone to all this trouble to have it made for her and had probably spent a ton of money on it. *What on earth?!* She had never seen something like this coming. Why couldn't they do something normal for a date, like a typical high-school couple would? Kirsten's Burger King date was sounding pretty appealing at the moment. It was nice dating someone who had a lot of money, but Aimee found herself wishing Josh was just someone normal that she had met in geometry class.

She stared down at the ID. Since she wasn't even old enough to own a driver's license yet, she didn't have a real ID on hand to compare to the fake, but upon first inspection it seemed authentic-looking. She racked her brain for something to say.

Josh didn't give her a chance. "Ready to go inside?"

"Are we just eating, or are we gambling?" There. That seemed like a safe question. She could probably justify it more if they were only using the IDs to get inside for the restaurant. It was still wrong, but a restaurant was a restaurant, whether it was in a casino or not.

He opened his car door and looked back at her, then

leaned over and placed his hand on her knee. "Aimee, relax. We're just eating. I wanted to try something different. There's supposedly a pretty epic buffet at Lochlomond's."

A buffet? They had driven all this way and Josh had purchased fake licenses so that they could eat at a buffet for an hour? Aimee didn't like Old Country Buffet, but right now it sounded like a much better option. She didn't want to protest leaving the car and look like a baby; she didn't want to call her parents to pick her up and have to defend herself to them; and she didn't want to use the fake ID.

She grabbed her purse and opened her car door. Josh was already standing at the front of the car, looking at her through the windshield. Obviously, he hadn't realized she would have such a problem with using a fake license. It reminded her of how little they really knew about each other and how everything about their relationship was much different than what she had figured having an almost-boyfriend would be like.

She silently followed him to the entrance. After twenty feet or so, he reached back and grabbed her hand. She tried to smile at the gesture but felt sick to her stomach about the IDs. A little ball of fury was building in her gut at Josh. Seriously? He hadn't even *asked* if she was okay with owning a fake ID before he'd had it created?

A few official-looking men with shiny nametags stood at the well-lit entrance to the casino, and Aimee watched nervously as they carefully inspected the IDs of the group of young people in front of her and Josh. Everything seemed to pass inspection, and they were waved on in. Aimee fumbled with her ID and nearly dropped it when the man closest to her reached for it. *Please look real, please look real.* Next to her, Josh seemed as cool as a cucumber and even chatted with the woman checking his birthday. Aimee studied the interaction, trying to understand how he could be so comfortable lying.

"Nice night, isn't it?" he asked, hands in his pockets and smiling widely.

"It's gorgeous," she responded, handing his ID back to him. "I heard it's supposed to be near eighty degrees tomorrow. You just never know what you're going to get in Michigan."

Aimee tried to appear confident and match Josh's smile as the guard glanced from the ID to her and back again. Finally he handed it back. "Have fun tonight," he said.

They were through! Aimee felt like she might faint as Josh gently took her elbow and guided her through the heavy glass doors. She was immediately overwhelmed as soon as they'd stepped just a few feet inside. For as far as Aimee could see, there were noisy slot machines with lights in all colors. Patrons were hitting buttons over and over again, staring at their machines and oblivious to what was going on around them. Some even looked like they were plugged into their slot machines, like gambling robots. She tried not to stare as Josh tugged her past an elderly gentleman with a cord clipped to his shirt pocket, the other end disappearing into his machine. He was smoking a fat cigar and only moved a single finger on one hand every few seconds to repeat his bet. Josh stopped a minute to place his ID in his wallet, and Aimee took the hint and carefully slid her own ID into her glittery wallet. A band played in a corner over to their left, and she craned her neck to see if it was anybody she recognized. Nope.

Aimee watched the table games with fascination as they passed them. She felt like she was in a James Bond movie (minus the fancy "casino wear" that seemed to dominate his movies). Josh held her hand the whole time they walked, and she was grateful for that connection, as all of the flashing lights and noise and groups of people made her feel lost in the establishment. She had a weird phobia that if Josh let go of her hand, she wouldn't be able to find her way outside on her own. As he pulled her closer to the wall, where the restaurants were lined up, she thought she caught a glimpse of someone she recognized. Could it be...? It was! It was the principal of her high school, Mr. Owens. He was sitting at one of the table games, playing in the same suit she'd seen him wearing earlier in the day when she'd passed him in the hall at school.

Oh, no. If he recognized her, he would probably realize she was not a senior, and therefore was not eighteen and too young to be in a casino. Of all the things that had darted through her mind when she realized Josh wanted her to enter a casino, running into someone she knew was not one of them. This was *horrible*.

She turned away quickly from the area where her principal sat, shock and panic gripping her. Mr. Owens hadn't glanced to his left at all, so he didn't realize she was there. It was imperative that she keep it that way.

"Josh," she said, tugging on his arm as they entered one of the restaurants.

"Table for two, please," he told the hostess, then turned to Aimee. "Yes?"

"My principal is here," she hissed, looking behind her even though at this point she couldn't see out into the gambling area anymore. That fact made her more nervous, because if Mr. Owens happened to decide to eat at this restaurant, too, he would round the corner into Lochlomond's without any warning. What if Aimee was accidentally looking his direction when he walked in? Would he alert the casino staff? Would she be thrown into juvie or something?

"Oh, really?" Josh finally looked nervous. He glanced up at the tiled entrance. "He's in here?"

"No, he's out there gambling." Aimee kept her eyes on the floor as the hostess led them to a table, scared to look around too much in case she saw anyone else she recognized. For all she knew, some of her friends' parents could be here somewhere, and they would definitely know that she wasn't old enough.

"How big is your school, though? Would he even recognize you?"

"Medium-sized. He might recognize me. I interviewed him last week for the school paper."

Josh pursed his lips but seemed determined to stay and follow through on their dinner plans. "I'm sure everything will be fine," he said.

The waitress took their drink orders and invited them to check out the buffet. As Aimee approached the massive spread, she had to acknowledge that Josh had been right. This was far more upscale than Old Country Buffet or any other buffet she'd ever visited. There was a beautiful section of raw fruit and vegetables, as well as some basic meats, like steak, that didn't have a ton of sauces on them, and she was excited to have so many healthy options.

Aimee took small pieces of chicken and steak and loaded up on fruit and vegetables. The plate was far fuller than any plate she'd eaten from in the last week, and despite the fact that she told herself she didn't care about calories anymore, Aimee mentally added up calories on her trek back to the table anyway. Although it still disturbed her that they were eating in a casino and she was underage, she had relaxed some now that they were away from the overwhelming sounds of the slots and the crowds of people who looked like zombies, zoned out in front of their individual machines. *We're only eating,* she justified. There was no law against teenagers eating in a restaurant.

But you used fake IDs to get in to this restaurant, her conscience argued.

But we're not going to gamble, she argued back. *Just quit worrying and enjoy this last night with Josh.*

During dinner, Josh asked her about various assignments she'd written for the school newspaper and whether she wanted to be a journalist when she graduated. She told him that she'd been thinking about it and hadn't decided for sure— that she wanted to continue to write articles for her high school paper and see if she kept enjoying it.

"Are you going to college after you graduate next year?" she asked him. Maybe if he was, he would move back to Michigan for college, and she would be able to see him more often.

"My parents want me to. I don't know, I really want to invent more games. I'm working on developing a new video game right now, and I think it could be a big success."

"That's cool," she said, genuinely fascinated by his creativity but also a little disappointed that he was thinking of skipping out on college. *Less chance of him moving back.*

She finished her full plate of food while they sat there and talked, and when Josh walked away to get a second plate, Aimee took in a deep breath and held her belly when she realized just how much she'd eaten and how full she was. *It was all healthy food, and not even that many calories,* she told herself. *You have no reason to feel bad about what you've eaten.* But for some reason she felt guilty, and she even found herself entertaining thoughts of ways to get rid of the food while Josh helped himself to lamb and mashed potatoes and gravy in the buffet line. Laxatives? Vomiting? No. First of all, she didn't have any laxatives, and the thought of sticking her finger down her throat to rid herself of a full plate of healthy food seemed disgusting and, quite honestly, scared her that she had even thought of it as an option. Her full stomach, which had barely contained any food the past week, felt like it was protruding grotesquely and made the waistband of her leggings drastically uncomfortable. She could just picture the massive indent she would find on the skin of her stomach from the leggings when she changed into her pajamas later that night. While Josh had his back turned to her at the buffet, she pulled at her waistband beneath the table to get a bit of relief.

He returned and took a seat. "Aren't you going to get any more food?"

Aimee smiled and shook her head. "No, I'm super full. It was really good, though."

Josh dug into the pile of potato salad on his plate. "I wish I didn't have to go back tomorrow." He kept looking down at his food instead of at her, leaving Aimee uncertain whether he meant he wished he could stay because of her, or whether he just meant in general that he wasn't ready to leave Michigan yet.

Aimee hesitated. Did she dare say the same thing and risk giving away the extent of her feelings for him? She didn't want to embarrass herself, so she replied, "When will you get to come back?"

"I'm not sure. Normally my family and I come back to Michigan to visit my grandparents every couple of months, but my grandma's not doing very well. My dad's talking about flying back in a couple of weeks this time."

Two weeks would go by quickly. Aimee pictured herself texting him between now and then. It would be okay. And it would give her a chance to decipher how she felt about potentially having a boyfriend who was an underage social smoker and saw nothing wrong with purchasing fake IDs to eat in a casino restaurant. Did he just like the thrill of doing something illegal without actually doing anything all that bad?

"How can you miss so much school?"

"I take the majority of my classes online. That way sometimes I can take an entire day off to work on things related to my video game, rather than only getting to do business on the weekends. Then I just catch up my schoolwork when I can. For example, I did a ton of reading for my history class on the plane to Michigan this time."

Aimee nodded and sipped her water.

"Are you sure you don't want anything else to eat?" he asked again. "I think I'm going to go grab some dessert."

Aimee suppressed a shudder at the thought of all of those sugary calories entering her body. She admired an ice sculpture of a swan near the ice cream section and said, "I really am full."

"Okay," he said reluctantly and stood up.

Sara

After the dishes were finished, Sara decided to distract herself from all of the calories she had consumed by checking her blog. She'd forgotten to get back to Ana's Servant over the weekend, so the girl was still waiting for an answer regarding whether or not Sara knew anybody personally who had died from anorexia. Sara hadn't wanted to dredge up that memory, but she had already shared it with her psychologist at their session that day, so why not answer this comment and be done with it? Tomorrow was a new day. She wrestled with how to keep things positive and yet tell the truth. Short and sweet was best, she supposed.

> **Hi Ana's Servant,**
> **Thanks for your comment! I wish I could tell you that I do not know anybody who has died from anorexia, but I don't want to lie to you. One of my best friends in high school, Rachel, died when she was just eighteen. The doctors said it was a heart attack caused by starvation. Rachel was one of the strongest anas I've ever known, and I still uphold her to this day as my role model for disciplining one's body. Be careful, though, that you diet in a smart way!**
>
> **Love,**
> **S.**

As Sara typed her tip for the day, "Pumping up the music will help you to forget about food and will make you lose the calories through dance" and compiled a quick top ten of food-forgetting dance songs, she debated whether or not to admit her larger-than-normal calorie consumption and share her counseling session with her blog audience. She also felt a small niggle of guilt over the fact that she had told Ana's Servant to diet in a smart way, which was a direct contradiction to all of the other advice she posted. How would Ana's Servant know how to diet in a smart way if the only blogs she was consulting were eating disorder ones? *It's not really my problem,* Sara consoled herself as she scrolled through new comments on last week's posts. *I didn't* make *the girl come to my site and read advice about severely restricting calories. I was polite and answered her question.*

That's all.

Aimee

Josh placed a tip on the table, and Aimee stood to pull on her coat. She had momentarily been able to forget about her principal's presence, but as they neared the doorway to enter into the gaming area again, she was gripped by the fear of being discovered to the point that she asked Josh to walk in front of her so she could hide behind him.

"I really think he probably won't recognize you, but I'll walk in front of you if you want me to," Josh said reluctantly.

"Thank you," she said, feeling stupid but also grateful that he agreed to her request. She couldn't risk her parents getting a phone call from her principal.

As they passed the table where Mr. Owens was playing poker, Aimee kept her head tucked down and eyes on Josh's heels, but a hearty laugh and loud cursing caused her to raise her head in curiosity. Her principal had fallen off his chair and was drunkenly trying to stand up. A helpful man finally took his hand and helped him to a standing position, where he stumbled again and nearly fell over but caught himself against the edge of the table. Aimee couldn't take her eyes off the scene. This was probably just one isolated incident, but it was definitely irresponsible behavior for the principal of a small-town school. On a school night, no less. Josh had also stopped and was staring openly at the man.

"I don't think you need to worry about him getting you in trouble. Looks like he's in a heck of a lot of trouble himself." Josh shook his head in disapproval.

Aimee nodded, shocked at the scene. Was she supposed

to tell someone that this was going on? Was this the type of thing that could get her principal fired? Even as she wondered about tattle-taling, she also acknowledged the fact that to save her own skin, she couldn't tell anyone. If she made such strong allegations about her principal's out-of-school behavior, people would want to know where she had seen him behave that way, and there was no chance she would share that particular piece of information. So she gritted her teeth, looked ahead, and pulled Josh by the hand toward one of the exits.

Once they were away from the main doors and in the middle of the parking lot, headed toward Josh's car, he laughed. "Aimee, you have nothing to worry about. Your principal had absolutely no idea you were there. He barely even knew *he* was there."

She nodded and tried to relax. Sure, she and Josh had just done something illegal, but their actions hadn't hurt anyone. It wasn't illegal to eat at a restaurant. They hadn't gambled at all. Josh seemed to have a strange addiction to doing things that were just barely illegal. The food had been delicious—she supposed she had enjoyed this date, but was it worth the risk of getting caught and getting in serious trouble? Aimee was used to following the rules and could only imagine what her parents would say if they knew that their rule-following daughter was being offered cigarettes and sneaking into casino buffets with a fake ID.

On the drive back, Josh pulled into a Dairy Queen and Aimee's stomach twisted in fear. What had happened to her in the past week to make her feel so afraid of junk food? No one was forcing it down her throat. She merely had to tell Josh she wasn't hungry, and she could get out of eating ice cream. As her mental calorie calculator kicked in, her heart rate rose higher and higher, picturing the fat from the ice cream bulging out from her stomach. No. She just couldn't eat any.

"Do you want some ice cream or a slushy or anything?" Josh asked as he pulled into the drive-through.

"No, I'm fine," Aimee squeezed out from her panicked throat. "Still full from dinner."

To her surprise, Josh swung out of the line without buying anything and pulled into a parking spot. He placed a hand on hers. "Aimee, before we head back to your house, I just wanted to tell you that I'm glad we met this weekend, and I'd like to see you again when I come back to Michigan. Would you be interested in getting together again? I'm hoping I'll be able to come back in a few weeks."

She should be excited. Aimee knew that every other "normal" girl her age would be thrilled that a handsome, wealthy boy was basically expressing that he wanted a dating relationship with her. Josh had been kind the past few days and had spoiled her. She had loved the attention and knew she should count her blessings that her first few dates ever had been a lot better than those many of her friends had experienced. He was a fun, intelligent guy. But did she want to continue to see someone who pushed her beyond the limits of what she felt comfortable doing? In just four days' time, she'd been asked to smoke and had been given a fake ID to sneak into an eighteen-and-older establishment. What would hanging out with Josh look like next time? Especially now that she had the fake ID?

On the other hand, she thought of her friends' wistful looks and sighs when she'd told them at lunch today about her time spent with Josh. "You're so lucky," they'd echoed each other, begging for more details about Josh's life and asking if she was going to take him to the dance with her. Aimee had been noncommittal but did allow herself to picture Josh dressed up in a suit, posing for pictures with her in a beautiful, shimmery dress, and holding her close while they danced together. She hadn't thought she wanted a relationship so badly until she had the chance to get involved in one.

The dance was in just under a month. If Josh came home again soon and things went well, maybe he would be able to be her date for the dance. If things didn't go well, she'd be back to being single for the dance, which had been her plan until this weekend anyway. No harm done.

"Yeah, I'd like to hang out with you again," she said, smiling.

Josh leaned over and kissed her on the cheek once more, his gaze darting to her lips as he pulled away. She blushed, tormented by the desire to lean in and let him kiss her on the mouth this time.

"Ready to go home?"

Not really, but she probably should. "Yeah, it's getting close to ten."

Once they were back on the highway, Josh reached over and grabbed her left hand. She squeezed his hand and leaned her head onto his right shoulder, leaving it there for the duration of the ride. She had to admit, it was really nice having someone like Josh be interested in her.

When they pulled into her driveway, Aimee lifted her head and dared to kiss Josh on the cheek. This was the first time she had made the first move, and he seemed to like it.

"See you in three weeks?"

She nodded. "See you then."

CHAPTER TWELVE

Aimee

As Aimee washed her face and got ready for bed after their date, she mostly pushed away her guilt at illegally entering a casino and instead concentrated on her drunken principal. She couldn't tell anyone about his behavior because she wasn't supposed to have been there, and she knew she shouldn't slander her principal, but man, this would make a great story for the school newspaper. Even if she wrote the piece, her teacher would surely reject it; but at the same time, didn't people need to know? It was one thing to act like that once, but if she had to guess, she'd say he was no stranger to heavy drinking in public. His behavior tonight combined with the email he'd sent her hinted at problems. He certainly was not representing their school well. How had the school district *not* found out? Basically, she'd need to catch him in the act again, in a location appropriate for her age. Probably the only way she could do that would be to follow him as he left school some evening. If only she had her driver's license instead of just a stupid permit…

She'd have to let someone in on this secret who could drive. She couldn't do it alone. Neither Coralee nor Meghan were sixteen yet, but wait! Meghan's birthday was in two weeks, and with her love of gossip, she would probably be up for a secret mission involving their principal. Aimee would most likely have to put off further investigation until then, as much as her curiosity begged to be satisfied. She spent the next ten minutes planning out how much information she was going to give Meghan and also what they would tell their parents to make this situation work.

Her phone chirped as she crawled into bed. She picked it up and saw a text from Josh.

Sleep well, babe.

She felt goosebumps at the term of endearment and grinned broadly. She knew she was falling for this guy and even though she questioned some of his life choices, Aimee was unsure if she could keep herself from contact with him.

She sent back a smiley face.

Good night.

She was almost asleep when she suddenly remembered the fake ID in her purse. She jumped out of bed and slid the license behind her dresser. No one in her family had any reason to move the heavy piece of furniture. It would be easy for someone to notice the license next time she opened her wallet if she left it there. Better safe than sorry.

Sara

Once Sara had answered Ana's Servant's question, the girl started acting as though she wanted to be Sara's new best friend. She began commenting on nearly every post of Sara's and, mixed in with some encouragement, also asked at least one or two questions every day. Sara popped in on Ana's Servant's blog every couple of days to read her updates and left her an occasional comment as well. Although Ana's Servant did not have a bio on her page, Sara figured the girl was most likely in high school, based on the way she wrote and the way her website was designed. This was by far the most interaction Sara had engaged in with any of her readers, and she had to admit that she enjoyed feeling like an expert on something. By now she had met with Dr. Renner a couple of times, and each time she returned home and sat down at the computer, she felt a little guiltier about continuing her blog. It appeared that the majority of her readers, including Ana's Servant, were young— probably around Aimee's age. Sara certainly wouldn't want Aimee to have access to information about how to endanger her health.

About ten days after the start of their online friendship, Ana's Servant abruptly stopped leaving comments on her page. Sara grew concerned—it wasn't just that Ana's Servant was suddenly ignoring her, but the fact that the girl was neglecting her own blog as well. Typically Ana's Servant had been updating her own blog two to three times per day, and suddenly Sara had heard nothing from her in over 48 hours, and neither had her blog audience. In light of the "death" question she had posed to Sara in their first conversation and what she claimed to weigh in her blog entries, Sara knew she was definitely in a danger zone. She wasn't the only one who had noticed Ana's Servant's absence—her loyal blog followers had begun posting a few comments on her last entry, requesting an update.

Aimee

With Josh absent from her life the next several days (other than occasional texts), Aimee spent more time on her anorexia article, investigating more blogs and attempting to craft something that would land her on the front page again. She was nervous to turn in her outline to Mrs. Bennett—would the teacher reject it and all of this research go to waste? She kept returning to the anorexia blog she had found early on in her research that appeared to be written by an older adult—most of the other blogs she'd found had been written by teens and college-aged students. Aimee also spent more time researching nutrition and trying to figure out the best way to keep herself at a healthy weight. She became alarmed at all of the information she turned up about how unhealthy various commonly-used ingredients were and how they were linked with causing various diseases.

On the days that she saw Mr. Owens in the hall, she took special note of his puffy face, red-rimmed eyes, and greasy, disheveled hair. Most of the time, he looked as though he'd barely awoken in time for work. There was still a chance he'd seen her at the casino. So as much as she wanted to inspect him as he passed her and maybe even glare at him a little for such disgusting behavior, she observed him from a ways off and kept her gaze down when they walked closer to each other.

The day she was supposed to turn in her outline, Mrs. Bennett was missing due to a family emergency and the substitute teacher said for the students to hang onto their outlines until Mrs. Bennett returned. Aimee felt both relieved and apprehensive that now she had to wait longer to see if her article idea would be accepted.

Two days before Meghan's birthday, Coralee stayed at home with strep throat. Aimee felt bad that her friend was sick but decided to seize the opportunity to ask Meghan about helping her follow Mr. Owens.

Aimee had started bringing lunch from home that week, since most days the salad bar looked completely unappetizing. When she had expressed interest in taking her own lunch to school, her mom had offered to pack it for her. Aimee was beginning to realize this was a bad idea, as Sara did not pack much of what Aimee now considered to be healthy. She took a seat at their usual table and unzipped her lunch pail to assess the health value of the contents while she waited for Meghan to get through the line.

Sandwich, apple, Cheetos, two miniature candy bars, and Gatorade. She pulled out the apple and lifted the top piece of bread on the sandwich to see if it was processed lunch meat or "real" meat. Definitely processed. Aimee sighed. No way could she eat that, with all of the nitrates that could possibly be included in the ingredient list. The only item that passed her inspection was the apple, so that was all she would consume for lunch.

She partially zipped her lunch back up before Meghan approached the table. She knew Meghan wouldn't understand why she was being so strict about food and didn't want to spend valuable lunch time explaining it. She had too many other things to discuss with her friend.

Meghan plunked her tray down across from Aimee and started in on her macaroni and cheese. Aimee nearly gagged at the unnatural yellowy-orange color. How had she never noticed these things until recently? She shuddered and swallowed the bite of apple in her mouth.

"Let me show you my dress for the dance!" Meghan whipped out her phone and displayed the sea green formal she'd picked up over the weekend.

Aimee nodded and smiled, still in limbo over whether she should ask Josh to come to the dance as her date. She hadn't mentioned the dance to him at all yet, and she hadn't gone shopping for the event, either.

"Did you buy a dress yet?"

"No. I don't know for sure if I'm going or not."

"Come on, just ask Josh! He obviously likes you. If you don't go shopping this weekend, we should go next week after I get my license!" Meghan grinned at her.

"Yeah...hey, Meghan, I have a question for you." Aimee drew in a deep breath. She didn't want to be a mooch to her friend, but if Meghan said no, she had no idea who to ask.

"Sure, what's up?"

Aimee leaned in and looked around to make sure no one was close enough to hear what she was about to share. "I have a story I want to scope out about Mr. Owens, but I need to be able to follow him after school." It was mostly true—she didn't know if she'd end up writing an article for the paper about Mr. Owens' problems or not, but she had to be careful what she told Meghan, since her friend had a few more days to spread information around before they did any real investigating.

Meghan cocked her head, and her eyes lit up. "What's going on?" she whispered.

Aimee bit her lip. "I can't tell you more right now, but I'll tell you next week. If I give you gas money, will you go with me to follow him after school sometime next week?"

"Definitely!"

Well, that was easy. As long as both sets of parents didn't mind the girls driving around by themselves, Aimee's plan would work.

Sara

When Sara returned home from running errands after dropping her kids off at school, she sat down in front of the computer. She only had one new comment on yesterday's post, but she hadn't expected it to be a wildly popular one, anyway. She scrolled down to check out the comment and gasped.

> **Who are you?! How can anyone live with herself who gives instructions to young girls on how to slowly starve themselves? My daughter is in the hospital right now because of you! She's in a coma! You'd better watch out, I'm going to find out who you are and take you to court.**

The commenter was logged in as Ana's Servant. Sara read through the message several times, trying to figure out if maybe Ana's Servant's account had been hacked. It had been a week now since Ana's Servant had left any new questions for Sara, and the girl had not updated her blog in the same period of time, either. Could there be a chance that this random comment was true information? She felt horrible about the girl's supposed illness, of course, but Ana's Servant had made her own choices. Sara certainly didn't force her to do anything or force her not to eat. And why had the girl's parent singled

Sara out? There were bound to be plenty of other blogs that Ana's Servant followed that all gave similar advice on calorie restriction. *What do I do?* Would this man or woman find a way to track her down? She'd never given out her real name on her blog, but could she be discovered through her computer's IP address? She had no idea how all of that techie type of stuff worked. She was just proud of herself for managing a blog on her own.

Sara began to cry thinking of how she would feel if Aimee was in a coma from purposeful starvation. She allowed memories of stick-thin Rachel in her pink casket to flood her brain. Why was she suddenly getting attacked after running this blog for over a year with zero problems? She was genuinely trying to get better by visiting Dr. Renner. She was consciously making an effort to begin eating normally again after more than half a lifetime of disordered eating. Should she tell her psychologist about this blog and about Ana's Servant? The thought made her head hurt. Should she delete this comment?

Yes. At the very least, she didn't want any of her other readers to see the offensive comment. *Best to get rid of it.* Maybe this person would leave her alone.

Aimee

Aimee spent the rest of the school day planning out in her head how she and Meghan could disguise themselves sufficiently. She didn't want the principal to know he was being followed. Once home, she picked out big sunglasses and a cute hat and texted Meghan so her friend would pick something similar.

Maybe she should wear something that made her look a

little older. Aimee rifled through her closet and pulled out the two blazers she owned. They were nice, but she needed something that screamed maturity. She headed downstairs to her parents' bedroom to check out her mom's closet. The bedroom door was mostly closed but not latched, her dad was still at work, and Aimee could hear someone moving around in the kitchen, so she figured no one was in the bedroom and didn't bother knocking. As she plowed into the room, her mom was just pulling a shirt over her head. Aimee stared in shock at her mother's ribs protruding beneath the band of her bra. Her stomach was sunken in, concave even, and her ribs almost looked sharp enough to cut through her skin. It took only a split second for her mom to finish getting dressed, and Aimee continued to stare at her mom's midsection even after it was covered by a baggy sweatshirt. The more she thought about it, the more she realized it had been a long time since she'd seen her mother's bare stomach. Her mom never went swimming, claiming to have a fear of the sport, and she always wore baggy, yet fashionable clothes, saying she wanted to look cool but be comfortable. Aimee figured the last time she'd seen her mom's midsection was the last time she'd seen her in a swimsuit, which was probably eight or ten years earlier. Sure, she hugged her occasionally and knew she was thin, but Sara never prolonged the hugs, so Aimee never got a good sense of how tiny she was.

"Aimee, what's up?" her mom asked calmly, and Aimee blinked to try to move her gaze up to her mom's face and away from the starvation horror she had just witnessed. She swallowed, trying to pretend like nothing was wrong.

"I was just wondering if I could look at your clothes. I...might borrow something, if that's okay."

"Sure, help yourself." In that instant, they heard "Oh no,

oh no," from the kitchen and grimaced at each other. "I have to go help Cody. He was just supposed to stir some sauce for me while I changed clothes, but it sounds like something happened."

Aimee nodded and stepped out of the way so her mom could squeeze past her. Except that her mom didn't really need to "squeeze," per se, in the narrow space. Aimee could see that she could fit quite easily with room to spare and wondered how she had never noticed that fact before.

What was going on? Was cancer wreaking havoc on her mom's body, and her parents hadn't even told Aimee and her brother yet? Was Sara about to lose her hair?

Who did she confront about this missing information? Her mom? She didn't want to embarrass her, so maybe her dad? If she brought it up to her mom, maybe Sara would feel self-conscious about the fact that she looked like a starving third-world child.

Aimee went to the closet and halfheartedly moved a few shirts around. Never mind. She would just wear something of her own. If the principal spotted her, he probably wouldn't recognize her anyway, just as he hadn't when they were at the casino.

She left the room and headed to the kitchen. Her mom was wiping up red sauce from the floor, while Cody wiped up red sauce from himself. With her mom on her knees like that, the fabric from her jeans pulled tight against her legs and Aimee could see just how thin her legs were—probably close to half the size of Aimee's legs. What was going on?

At dinner (spaghetti), Aimee thought about all of the fat in the meatballs and only ate one, along with a few noodles (whole wheat) and a salad with no dressing. She watched her mother carefully and picked up on things she had never noticed before—her mom's eating habits. Sara spent much of the meal asking her husband and the two kids questions and would set down her fork when she was talking and while listening to everyone's responses. She would only pick up her fork again once the entire table was quiet. Although she had some spaghetti on her plate, the only thing Aimee saw her actually take bites from was her salad, which had no dressing. Her mom pushed the spaghetti around a few times, severed through long noodles with her fork, and cut up the meatballs into tiny pieces. But as far as Aimee could tell, her mom never took a bite of the main entree.

That night, Josh called Aimee at 7:30. He told her the time his flight would be arriving in Michigan the following week and told her about the new video game, Grimm Tales, he had been busy creating. Aimee uttered the proper "yeah"s and "oh, man"s, but she could really only think of what might be wrong with her mom. Finally, when Josh asked her how she was doing, Aimee spilled her guts, hoping he would give her some perspective and assure her everything was probably fine.

"Josh, I'm concerned my mom might be seriously ill," she whispered, glancing toward her bedroom door to make sure it was closed. "Today I accidentally walked in on her while she was getting dressed, and she was *so skinny*. Like, I could almost count her ribs she was so thin. And tonight she barely ate anything at dinner, just salad, and the more I think about it, she's been getting a lot of headaches lately, and...what if she has cancer or a brain tumor or something and my parents just haven't told anyone?"

Josh snickered. "Gross. You walked in on your mom while she was getting dressed?"

Aimee glared at him through the phone even though he couldn't see her. "It was an accident; I didn't realize she was in her bedroom. That's all you got out of what I just said?!"

"Why don't you just ask her if she's okay?" he said, sounding impatient.

"Well, I can't word it like that; of course she's going to say she's okay," Aimee retorted. "I don't know, maybe I should ask my dad. I don't want my mom to think that I think she's ugly for being so thin or something."

"Whatever. I think you're overthinking things," Josh said, and she heard him breathe deeply.

"What are you doing? Are you walking or something while we're talking?" Aimee said, instantly suspicious.

"No, I'm sitting still. Why, babe?"

Her mood softened a little when he called her that, but she stood her ground. "You were breathing funny."

"Oh, I'm just...just smoking," he confessed.

"I thought you only did that once in a while, around friends. Are you with friends right now?"

There was silence on the other end of the line. "No. I'm at home."

"Well, is it just a cigarette, or is it pot or something?" *Please say just a cigarette.* But she was growing more and more suspicious, considering that he seemed unable to be sympathetic to her situation.

"It doesn't matter, Aimee. I'm aware enough to hold a conversation; isn't that what's important?"

Aimee wanted to scream. "No. I don't want to date someone who does drugs, Josh!"

"Aimee, calm down, I—"

"I think we need to call it a night, Josh. I'll talk to you some other time."

"Aimee, wait—"

She ended the call. She knew she should probably break

up with him, but she also knew she didn't want to have to face that truth right now. Not when she could be facing a life-and-death situation with her mom. She decided to come up with the perfect plan for talking to her parents and then approach them both on the subject sometime in the next few days.

Meghan had decided to postpone her birthday party until the following weekend so that Coralee would be healthier and would be able to attend. Aimee spent the weekend at home and tried desperately to connect with her parents on the topic of Sara's health, but Cody ended up with extra soccer games, and her dad had to help with an event at church. There never seemed to be a time where both Sara and Dave were available to talk without Cody listening in.

Monday was the day Aimee and Meghan had agreed on to follow their principal. Aimee carried her hat and sunglasses in her bookbag and met Meghan at her car immediately after school.

Neither of them had any idea what time the principal would be leaving for the day. For all Aimee knew, she and Meghan would be waiting two hours for him. While they sat in Meghan's car and waited, the two girls put on their "disguises," and Meghan pressured Aimee for more details regarding the reason for following Mr. Owens.

"I—I can't tell you how I know this, but Mr. Owens might be an alcoholic."

"Why can't you tell me how you know it? Is it just based on that email or what? I'm one of your best friends! You know I won't tell anybody if it's something that needs to be kept a secret." Meghan slouched in her seat and crossed her arms over her chest.

"I know, but…" Aimee clasped her hands together and faced her friend. "Just trust me. It's better that you don't know."

"If we can confirm that it's true today, will you tell me then?"

Aimee was silent for a moment. Meghan loved gossip, and Aimee certainly did not need the news of her fake ID spreading all over the school. But Meghan was spending all this time helping her, and she probably did deserve some kind of a reward for giving up her afternoon and evening for Aimee's project.

Aimee sighed and gave in. "If we can confirm that his alcoholism is a real thing today, I will tell you how I knew, and I will also buy you lunch this weekend."

Meghan's face grew into a satisfied smile. "Thank you," she said smugly.

They did not have to wait long for the principal to make an appearance. Just after 3:30, he stepped out into the sunshine and headed for the teachers' parking lot. He had a leather pouch tucked under one arm.

"It looks like he's going to make a bank deposit or something." Aimee buckled her seatbelt and sat up straighter.

They waited until his car had begun to reverse, then Meghan quickly started up her engine and began to pull out of her own spot. They followed him a short ways to downtown, where sure enough, he pulled into a parking spot in front of the bank. They parked several spots away and waited for him to come back out. Ten minutes later, he returned, bank bag tucked under his arm, and his open wallet in the other hand. He was stuffing cash into his wallet.

"I think he might be heading to the casino!" Aimee squealed, barely able to contain her excitement that she was right.

"Or he might just be taking money out to buy groceries

or give his kids their allowance or something." Meghan was unconvinced.

"True."

Aimee remained quiet as they followed the principal onto the highway. He headed south (one more point for casino!) and acted as though he was in a hurry. Meghan had to constantly change lanes and speed to keep up with him. At one point she was going close to 85. "I had better not get a ticket during my first week as a licensed driver," Meghan mumbled angrily. "This had better be worth it."

The girls car-danced their way through half an hour of Ariana Grande and Taylor Swift songs until Mr. Owens finally took the exit for the casino. They followed him into the parking lot, turned the opposite direction of him, and were able to find a spot where they could watch the front entrance without too much trouble. They waited two minutes as he jogged up to the double doors, looking eager to get inside. Despite the fact that he actually looked quite young for his age, the security men at the door didn't bother to card him. In fact, they waved at him as if they recognized him—another fact that troubled Aimee and convinced her that her suspicions might be accurate.

Once he was inside, Meghan set her phone down (she had been taking video footage of the principal entering the casino) and stared at Aimee. "You really might be right on this. Are you going to tell me yet why you suspected something might be up with him?"

"No." Aimee shook her head. "Let's just see what happens."

They had waited two and a half hours before Meghan announced she had to go to the bathroom. "Let's just go down the road a ways and use the bathroom at Taco Bell. I can see the sign from here."

"What if we miss him exiting the casino?" Aimee whined. Her bladder was bothering her, too, but she didn't want to miss out on his drunken exit.

"We'll be gone five minutes. From what you've said, I think he'll be in there a while longer, Aimee. Honestly, we can't stay a lot longer. Our parents will be wondering where we are. After all, I told my mom I should be home by eight."

Aimee had told her mom the same thing, and it was already nearing 7:30. "Okay, let's make a quick stop at Taco Bell and then come back. Can you call your mom and tell her you'll be a little later?"

"I guess so. It's her car, though, so I don't know what she'll say."

"Okay. Let's go to the bathroom, come back and watch for a bit, and then we'll head home."

"Agreed."

After visiting the facilities, Meghan bought a freeze, and the two returned to camping out in the parking lot. Aimee texted her mom while Meghan left her own parents a voicemail to let them know there would be a delay. When Sara asked what they were up to, Aimee hesitated for a couple of minutes. While she deliberated over the best answer, their principal staggered out the front doors of the casino. Meghan excitedly pulled out her phone again to record his behavior. "Is he going to drive himself home like that?"

Aimee shrugged. She sure hoped not, but it looked that way. *Should we step in?*

It was too late. He'd already started his car. The girls followed him out of the parking lot. It was clear they didn't need to be as careful when following him home—there was no way he was aware enough of what was going on around him to notice two of his students in the car behind him. He would swerve occasionally, and the cars in the oncoming lane would honk angrily. Aimee contemplated calling the police and reporting him.

They were nearly home when Owens made yet another swerve into the opposite lane, this time in front of a tiny smart car. The driver honked, but it was too late. Mr. Owens smashed into the car, stepping on his brakes only *after* impact, and the girls witnessed airbags exploding in both vehicles. Shards of metal and glass flew in every direction, including onto Meghan's windshield, as Meghan slammed on her brakes to avoid hitting either vehicle. The girls winced when something heavy crunched against the roof of their car. Aimee was unbuckling her seatbelt to get out and help the victims when all of a sudden Owens reversed a little, scraped the front bumper of Meghan's car, and drove away from the scene.

"What???!!!" the girls yelled together. The airbag in the smart car had deflated, and they could see that the driver was motionless inside.

Aimee quickly dialed 911, jumping out of the car at the same time as Meghan.

They hurried over to the smart car, but the doors were so damaged that they couldn't get inside to help the woman. They could hear her moaning, and they tried to encourage her that an ambulance was coming as they listened to the sirens approaching.

The first responders ended up having to use the Jaws of Life to extricate the woman from the car. By the time they got her out, she'd stopped moaning and seemed to be having trouble breathing. The police were preoccupied with helping to get the woman out of the car, but as soon as the ambulance had taken off, they turned to the teens to try to get some answers.

"Did you see what happened?" the older officer asked.

Meghan and Aimee looked at each other and drew in deep breaths. Aimee dove in first.

"Yes. It was our principal who hit her. He was drunk."

As she and Meghan both shared more details and Aimee carefully avoided the reason she had decided to follow their principal in the first place, she thought about the possibility that she might have to go to court and wondered how she would avoid mentioning her fake ID. As the policemen were wrapping up the interview, a news van parked nearby.

"I don't want to talk to the news," Aimee blurted out.

The officer nodded. "That's a good idea. We don't want to give them too much information until we've tracked down Mr. Owens and questioned him. You girls go on home and we'll be in touch."

Aimee and Meghan spun around and headed back to their car. Although the windshield was cracked and they needed to haul a chunk of metal off of the top of the vehicle, it was still drivable. Aimee was beginning to feel lightheaded. There had been so much excitement and very little food in her stomach the past few weeks. On that particular day, she'd only eaten some blueberries for breakfast and then an apple for lunch. It was far past her usual dinnertime, and she really just needed to get home and relax.

They were within ten feet of Meghan's car when a reporter bounded up, cameraman following close behind. "Girls! Did you cause the accident? Did you see what happened? Tell us what you saw!"

Aimee's heart leapt at the verbal attack, and she spun around to look for the officer to get the reporter away from their faces. As she did so, her dizziness increased, and she felt herself tipping to the side, then everything blacked out.

CHAPTER THIRTEEN

Aimee

When Aimee awoke, she was lying in a hospital bed. Her mom was stroking her hand, and her dad was talking to Cody quietly in a corner of the room.

"Honey, how do you feel?" her mom asked as soon as Aimee opened her eyes.

"My head hurts," she moaned, lifting a hand to touch her face. An IV line trailed along with her hand.

"You passed out and hit it on the asphalt." Her mom stared at her with worried eyes, and Aimee remembered her concern over her mom's health. She was feeling a little drugged up and couldn't stop herself from asking, "Mom, are you sick?"

Sara looked shocked. "No, why do you say that, honey?"

"You're getting so thin, and you're so pretty, but you're so thin. I thought maybe you had cancer or something." Aimee began to cry. Her mom was looking out for her, but who was looking out for her mom?

"No, honey. I don't have cancer." Sara looked nervous and glanced over at her husband. He nodded and offered to Cody that they should go get a snack in the cafeteria.

Cody looked from their father back to Sara. "You're okay, Mom?" He looked worried.

Sara smiled reassuringly. "I'm fine, sweetie. Go get something to eat."

He nodded and followed their father out into the hall.

"What's going on, then?" Aimee was not going to be deterred.

"Honey, before I tell you what's going on with me, I need to ask you some questions. Why haven't you been eating very much?"

"I've been eating, just trying to make healthier choices. Why are you changing the subject?" The anger was trying to build up inside, but it only made her head hurt more. Aimee attempted to relax her face to ease the throbbing sensation. Immediately after answering Sara, she wondered if what she had said was true. Yes, she'd been eating…but after all the time she'd spent studying anorexia and proper nutrition, she supposed she'd been leaning more toward the anorexic side of things. Well…she just needed her mom to buy more healthy options for meals and snacks was all. There was no way she was anorexic.

"The doctors needed to run some tests because you passed out. A lot of your tests indicated that your body isn't getting enough nutrition—that you're not eating enough food." Sara was crying now, too. "Why aren't you eating? Did you learn that from me?"

"Learn what from you?" All of a sudden, it clicked. Aimee couldn't believe she hadn't picked up on the signs earlier with all of the research she had done.

"Aimee, I'm going to tell you something I've tried to hide from you all my life." Sara drew in a deep breath. "I've struggled with anorexia for the past twenty years. I've had some stretches where I returned to eating healthy, but for the most part I have been restricting myself, and that's why I'm so thin. I never wanted you and Cody to be concerned about your own weight, though, so I tried to make sure I provided you with plenty of healthy food so you wouldn't turn out like me."

"Well, are you going to go see a psychologist or something?" Aimee asked. "I-I don't want you to die." She sniffed.

"I am already seeing one. I might be going away to an eating disorder clinic soon, though." Sara looked down and away from her daughter.

The pamphlet! It hadn't been for Aimee…they hadn't even realized what was going on with Aimee until now. Aimee still wasn't convinced she was doing anything wrong for her body; she was simply eliminating junk food and making healthy choices.

"Aimee, I think…I think you might need to go to the clinic with me, too."

Aimee exploded. "What? Why? I'm eating, Mom."

"How many calories a day have you been eating, Aimee?"

"I don't know." She didn't know exactly, but the more she thought about it, the more she realized the level she had been at was probably dangerous.

"I think you do know. I can tell you exactly how many calories I've eaten today—210." Sara was being extra honest and bold.

"Yeah. I've probably been eating anywhere from about 500 up to 1200 a day."

"That's not enough for a teenage girl."

Aimee nodded.

"Aimee, I don't want your life to turn out as controlled by food as mine has been. If I go to that clinic, will you go with me?"

Aimee closed her eyes. "I'll think about it."

When her mom stepped out of the room for a while, Aimee was able to check her phone. She was surprised to see a text from Josh.

Aimee, I heard you were in a car accident! Are you okay?

Who would have told him that?

She rubbed her face with one hand while staring at the screen. Should she talk to him at all? Despite how rude he had been during their most recent conversation, she still sort of wanted to be his girlfriend. What was *wrong* with her?

Aimee sighed and gave in to the urge to answer Josh's text.

No, I wasn't exactly in a car accident. I just got hurt. I'm in the hospital, but I'm okay now.

His response came quickly.

What hospital?

She didn't want to tell him and risk a visit while she looked so awful. She wasn't sure if he was back in town or not. She wasn't even completely sure what day it was anymore. Aimee set the phone aside and fell asleep.

*****

"Special delivery." A nurse woke Aimee up to check her vitals and gently waved a huge vase of flowers in front of her. "A young man dropped these off for you at the nurses' station."

Aimee struggled to sit up and took the tiny card that was tucked in among pink and white roses.

Hope you get well soon. Text me if you'd like a visitor.

Josh

The nurse offered to set them on a nearby side table, and Aimee nodded. She bit her lip and read the few words on the card over and over before the nurse finally had to remind her that she needed Aimee to give her an arm to check her blood pressure.

A few hours later, she finally texted him:

Thanks for the flowers

She was released from the hospital the next day, and before she left, a doctor talked to her and her parents for nearly an hour about options for healing from eating disorders. He explained to Aimee that while she may not be anorexic, she might be struggling with something she hadn't realized existed—orthorexia. As he described that orthorexia involved a fear of eating unhealthy foods, Aimee realized that perhaps her thoughts about food had become too controlling. The kicker came when Sara opened up about her own eating disorder more, and Aimee realized that she didn't want to live the way her mom had been—she wanted to enjoy food (while eating healthy most of the time) and not be afraid of occasional junk food. She decided she would go to the eating disorder clinic with Sara. It would definitely help prevent potential harm in her own body, and she could be a support to her mom while there.

*****

When Aimee arrived home from the hospital and was left alone in her bedroom to rest, she wrestled back and forth with what to do about Josh. After her thank-you text, he had tried to start a conversation, but she hadn't responded. She appreciated his concern and part of her wanted to continue their friendship/relationship/whatever it was, but he kept putting her in such uncomfortable situations. So finally Aimee just poured her energy into packing, because she and her mom were leaving for the eating disorder clinic at the end of the week.

Would it be hot? Cold? They were headed to Tennessee. She pulled up the weather forecast and, out of habit, checked on some of the anorexia blogs for updates. One of them was the blog that appeared to be written by an older adult. As she spent a little time on the site, she noticed some details that she hadn't picked up on previously. Some things like "Favorite Dance Songs for Burning Calories" and what the blogger had eaten in the past few days seemed familiar. Could it be…? No, when would her mom have time to write blog posts? But wow…some of those songs were definitely played frequently in their house, and it didn't seem possible that the author's meals that week had been so similar to those served at Aimee's house. Even the main color theme of the blog—varying shades of purple—matched up with her mom's favorite color. Aimee clicked on the comments under the most recent entry.

I saw that you deleted my previous comment. You can't get rid of me that easily. My daughter is still in the hospital. I've got a lawyer, and I'm going to find out who you are.

Aimee read the comment through several times. If this really was her mom's blog, it sounded as though Sara could be in serious trouble.

"Mom!"

A minute later Sara appeared in the doorway. "Yeah?"

"Is this your blog?" Aimee watched the color drain from Sara's face as she stepped closer to view the screen. She looked scared when she read the comment.

Sara cleared her throat. "Yes. How did you find this?"

"I came across it when I was looking at other blogs about anorexia. I found it a few weeks ago but didn't think it might be yours until now. Are you going to have to get a lawyer or something? What happened?"

Sara shook her head. "Some girl has been contacting me for advice, and now all of a sudden someone—supposedly her parent—is accusing me of making that girl sick because she apparently followed my dieting advice. They left one comment a few days ago, and I deleted it. I had hoped it was just spam or something. I guess not."

"Does Dad know?"

"He doesn't know about my blog." Sara bit her lip. "Don't worry, Aimee, I don't think they can take me to court for something like this. I always put on my entries that I'm not a doctor and that people should not look to me for medical advice. I'm sure my blog isn't the only one that the girl was following for diet information, anyway." Her worried face contradicted her assurances. "I'll talk to your father about it." Sara patted Aimee on the back. "Keep working on packing. I'm going to go finish making dinner."

Despite her mom's words, Aimee did not return to packing immediately, but instead kept reading through Sara's old blog entries. They had started out as only one or two entries per week a year ago, but in the last month her mom had posted as many as five times per week. She cried when she read how many calories her mom typically consumed and wondered how she had never noticed the symptoms.

CHAPTER FOURTEEN

Sara

Sara forced herself to eat a few bites of each item on her plate at dinner, but this time she was having trouble eating for a reason other than her anorexia. Despite the fact that she'd tried to reassure Aimee that everything would be okay with her blog, she certainly didn't know for sure. On top of being worried about getting sued and mounting guilt about possibly having something to do with Ana's Servant's illness, she now had to work up the courage to introduce Dave to her blog after dinner.

It was the kids' once-a-week turn to put the leftovers away after supper and do dishes, but for once Sara wished she had never started that rule. She wanted to procrastinate on talking to Dave about this issue for as long as possible.

David had stepped into the living room to watch the news after dinner, and Sara waited to join him until the rush of running water and clatter of plates and silverware was loud enough to help cover up their voices. Finally, she quietly slipped into her usual chair next to him and took a few deep breaths to calm herself. "Dave?"

He blinked at her sleepily and set the TV remote on the arm of his chair. "Hmmm?"

"I need to tell you something." Sara's voice started out with a quiver but gradually gained strength as she explained her blog situation. "I don't know what to do. Do you think they can actually sue me for this? I never meant to hurt anybody. I thought I was being careful by writing on my entries that people shouldn't consult me for medical advice because I'm not a doctor, but I guess I don't put that on one-on-one correspondence with people. And I keep picturing Aimee in her hospital bed, and how scared I was when I found out that she had been eating so restrictively like me, and I feel awful if I caused another family to have to go through something similar..." Her last words came out in a rush and two tears slipped from the corner of her eye. "Dave, I'm scared."

Her husband had gone pale. "Sara. This is a big deal. You've been telling other people how to be anorexic?!"

"I-I—I guess you could say it that way, yes." Sara looked down at her hands and started picking her fingernails. "It's a whole community online, and when I first found out about it, I was excited. It was nice to connect with some people like me. But I hadn't realized how harmful it was until the last few weeks." Another tear trailed off her chin and dripped onto her thumb. "What do I do? Should I contact a lawyer? How expensive is that? Can we afford it?" It was a struggle to keep her voice low so that their children wouldn't hear. The panic was growing, a big monster squeezing her lungs and trying to make her scream in fear.

"You meet with Dr. Renner tomorrow, right?"

She nodded. It would be her last appointment with the

psychologist before she and Aimee left for Tennessee.

"Talk to her and see what she recommends. I think we're going to have to get a lawyer." Dave ran a hand through his hair. Several strands stood up wildly. "I'll ask around at work tomorrow and see if anybody knows a good one."

"You won't tell them what the lawyer is for, will you? They'll think I'm crazy."

"No, I won't give them much information." Dave rested a hand on her cheek. "You're not crazy, by the way. We all have problems. You're being brave and getting help for your problem. I'm proud of you." He kissed her, leaned his head back on the chair, and rubbed his eyes. "I love you, Sara. We'll get all of this figured out, but it might take a while."

She stood up and hugged him. "Love you, too, Dave. Thank you."

Aimee

After finishing up the dinner dishes with Cody, Aimee sorted through the pile of mail on the counter to see if there was anything for her. She was surprised to find an important-looking envelope and opened it. There was a subpoena inside summoning her to court to testify against her principal in the hit-and-run accident. She immediately texted Meghan.

Do you have to go to court for Mr. Owens?

Yes ☹ I don't want to.

Me either.

Maybe you won't have to go because you'll be in TN?

Maybe. I don't think it works that way, though.

Aimee read through the paperwork twice before approaching her parents. If she had to go to court, did that mean she would end up having to tell everyone—including the *judge?*—that she had used a fake ID to enter a casino illegally? What would happen then? *I can't believe I let Josh talk me into going into the casino. Now I'm the one dealing with the consequences, and he's off the hook. I sort of wish I'd never followed Mr. Owens back to the casino. Maybe somebody else would have witnessed the crash that way, and I wouldn't be involved in this situation at all.*

She found her dad in the living room, half-awake and groggily watching the news. "Dad, I need to show you something that came in the mail."

"Huh?" He turned to her and held out a hand for the paperwork. He adjusted his bifocals as he skimmed the subpoena. "I'm sorry, Aimee. I thought this might be coming. I know it's a pain, but you want to help the lady he hit, right?"

"Of course. It's not really the idea of going to court that scares me; it's more what I might have to talk about at court and whether I'll get in trouble." Aimee pulled her hair into a ponytail to buy herself a few more seconds to think of the best way to admit her guilt.

Dave squinted at her. "Aimee, you won't get in trouble. Why would you think that?"

She shrugged. "I might. You don't know the whole situation."

"Okay. Fill me in." He removed his glasses.

Aimee dove into the story of the casino and, even though

the gaming night didn't have anything to do with testifying against Mr. Owens, she spilled the truth about Josh and his friends smoking as well.

Her dad looked somewhat overwhelmed, and that expression did not help Aimee's hope that everything would be okay. "Aimee, first of all, I'm proud of you for not smoking. But I never would have thought that you would use a fake ID."

Aimee shook her head. "Me, either."

"So you really didn't gamble when you were inside? You guys just ate at one of the restaurants and left?"

"Yeah. And that was when I saw Mr. Owens acting all drunk. So do you think that's going to come up when I have to go to court for him?"

Dave cringed. "I think it's possible, yes. Aimee, I appreciate your honesty, but you do realize I'm going to have to punish you for using the fake ID, right? I'm not sure what will happen if you admit it in court, but there will definitely be some sort of punishment here at home. I'll have to talk about this with your mom." He shook his head. "If you start having any second thoughts about seeing Josh again, you can forget about it. You're not allowed to hang out with him anymore. I should have gotten to know him better before you were allowed to go out with him, anyway. I was distracted with figuring out what to do about your mom's health, and I'm sorry for not checking the situation out better. Thank you for being honest."

Aimee nodded, slightly frustrated that she was going to be punished (she had told her father the truth, after all, and had no intention of using the ID ever again) but also somewhat relieved that her dad had given her the push to stay away from Josh. She left the living room and dug the fake ID out from behind her dresser. Grabbing a pair of scissors, she cut it up into the wastebasket beside her desk. Now all she could do was make an awkward call to Josh while she waited for the verdict on how her parents were going to handle her poor decision.

Josh answered on the second ring. "Aimee! I hated how we left our last conversation. I'm really sorry for how I acted last time we talked."

Aimee sighed and gritted her teeth, torn between her mushy heart and the knowledge that she would be disobeying her parents if she continued to see him. "Josh, thanks for your apology, but I don't think we should hang out anymore. I've had fun with you, but I can't be with someone who pushes the limits all the time like you do. It's stressful, and I don't want to live my life like that."

There was silence on the other end, and then a click. *Really? He didn't say anything? Good riddance to his immaturity.*

One tear dripped off her chin as she sniffed and returned to evaluating the contents of her suitcase.

Sara

Sara was startled by Dave's revelation that Aimee had used a fake license. He shared the information with her while they were laying in bed the next night, unable to sleep due to all of the stress that had been mounting over the past few days.

"The good news is that I did get some tips about lawyers today," he said. "Now I'm thinking we'll need one for you and your blog, as well as to defend Aimee because I don't know how she's going to be able to avoid telling about the casino when she's asked to share why she and Meghan were following their principal in the first place. This is going to be expensive, Sara."

"We can wait to go to Tennessee," she offered. "I mean, I know that's not ideal, but if we have to…"

"No. You and Aimee are going." Dave's voice was firm in the darkness. "I don't know how we're going to pay for everything, but yours and Aimee's health are important. We're still leaving on Sunday."

EPILOGUE

Aimee

Aimee slid her swimsuit up and over her hips and smiled in the mirror. She and her mom had returned home two weeks ago after a nine-week stay at the eating disorder clinic. Since she was new to struggling with food, Aimee's program would not have taken as long; however, due to her family history of problems, the staff decided to keep her as long as her mother was there. She felt as though she had a much better grasp on proper nutrition and exercise than she had before her time at the clinic, and she was the most pleased with her body that she had ever been. Sara was having a more difficult time adjusting to their new lifestyle, but she had gained a few pounds over the course of their stay, and the counselors gave Aimee some tips on how to continue to help her mom once they arrived back home. The two were also going to begin attending a local weekly support group.

Aimee and Meghan were scheduled to testify in three days regarding the Owens case. The lawyer Dave had hired said he suspected that Aimee's punishment for using a fake license would be small, since she hadn't gambled and since her testimony would help convict Mr. Owens. She was still a little nervous. Regardless of what punishment the court doled out to Aimee, her parents had decided that their punishment for her would be grounding for six weeks, along with extra chores around the house during that time. Aimee had suffered through one-third of her punishment so far and could not wait for the end of it so that she could get her driver's license and hang out with Meghan and Coralee.

She had dutifully kept up with her schoolwork while in Tennessee and, after much consideration, had even finished her anorexia article and submitted it to Mrs. Bennett. Her teacher was somewhat concerned about giving other students ideas on how to restrict their eating but thought that Aimee's brave decision to include how her experiment had spiraled out of control, resulting in a hospital stay and out-of-state treatment, would serve as a warning to teens who may be toying with an eating disorder.

The whole family was starting to relax about the accusatory comments on Sara's blog. A few days after Sara and Aimee's arrival in Tennessee, Dave notified them that Ana's Servant had begun posting on her own blog again (he was keeping an eye on that situation since it was, of course, frowned upon to view such content while at the clinic). Ana's Servant's parents had not commented on Sara's blog for three months now, and Sara was relieved that it appeared her loyal admirer had not needed any subsequent trips to the hospital. The girl's posts indicated that she was genuinely trying to heal from her eating disorder.

As Aimee gathered up her towel to go outside and tan on their back deck (a celebration of the fact that she had just emailed in her last homework assignment of the school year), her phone dinged. She hadn't heard from Josh since she'd broken up with him, but all of a sudden, here was a text from him.

Aimee, I'm going to be in town this weekend. I know we ended on a bad note, but I do miss you and wondered if you would like to get together on Saturday.

"Aimee?"

Aimee looked up as her mom approached.

"Will you help me with something before you head outside?"

"Yeah." She followed Sara to the family computer and saw her mom's blog on the screen.

"I want to delete my blog." Although Sara's voice wavered as she spoke, the look she gave her daughter was firm. "But I don't know how."

"Oh. Okay." Aimee sat in the desk chair and played around on the computer for a couple of minutes before locating the information her mother needed to complete her plan. "Are you sure?"

Sara nodded. "I've got to do it now before I lose my nerve."

"All right." Aimee moved out of the way so her mom could get to the mouse. "Here you go."

Sara took a deep breath and clicked to confirm that she wanted to delete *Shh—I Don't Eat*. A tear slid onto her cheek as she smiled.

Aimee hugged her mom. "Good job, Mom. You did the right thing."

"Love you, Aimee."

"I love you, too." She walked out into the hall to continue on her way to the deck but stopped long enough to send an answer to Josh.

No.

Also written by Angela:

Illegally Innocent

Made in the USA
Lexington, KY
17 July 2017